THE *Singing*

Theron Raines

A Morgan Entrekin Book

The Atlantic Monthly Press

New York

THE *Singing*

A Fable About What
Makes Us Human

Published simultaneously in Canada
Printed in the United States of America
First edition

Library of Congress Cataloging-in-Publication Data
Raines, Theron.
   The singing: a fable about what makes us
human.
   "A Morgan Entrekin book."
   I. Title.
PS3568.A423S56   1988   813'.54   87-30721
ISBN 0-87113-177-3

Design by Julie Duquet

The Atlantic Monthly Press
19 Union Square West
New York, NY 10003

First Printing

To Joan

To search for perfect love is a mistake,
at least so far as reason holds a place
in how we build our lives and how we take
the little disappointments of our case.
A perfect object has no worth at all
unless some lover perfect hold it so
and raise around his love an ivory wall,
a moral prison where no love can grow.
Myself imperfect, prizing what I've found,
the heart of you in these few years together,
I lay my claim to this enchanted ground
and write a garden where sweet spirits gather.

    May scarecrow story work a spell of words,
    confounding time, which flickers off like birds.

THE *Singing*

*S*PINOZA SAYS THAT ACCIDENT
OR CHANCE IS THE NAME WE GIVE
TO AN EVENT WHOSE CAUSES WE
DO NOT UNDERSTAND.

Mary Alice sat at the typewriter paralyzed and furious, her fingers poised over
the keyboard. The next phrase simply
refused to come, and she gazed dumbly at
the headline, knowing she would *never*
write a decent piece of copy to follow it.
She had jotted down the Spinoza idea yesterday as a campaign theme for a casino
that would open next fall in Atlantic City.
The casino was called 1001 Nights and
promised a $3 million account—if the
agency came up with a campaign to make

this new place stand out from the dozen others already lining the Boardwalk.

The client, a giant fat man with a chirpy little voice like a canary, had said he wanted an upscale tone: ". . . something like Rolls-Royce and, *tsk,* Piaget." With a car or a wristwatch you could buy an elegant illusion about yourself, but why, Mary Alice wondered, did people go to casinos? What was the gambler *buying?* Yesterday the quote from Spinoza had made her feel positively inspired, but today she was flat, flat, flat. The whole morning was gone, and nothing usable had come to her.

But wait a minute! She had written the headline as a statement—and it was really a quotation. How would it look inside quote marks, and in italics rather than caps? She pulled out the sheet, rolled in fresh paper, and typed:

> *"Accident or chance is the name we give to an event whose causes we do not understand."*—B. Spinoza.

She read the lines over, pondered a moment, and X'ed out the *B.,* then looked at it again. Her hopes fell; it was no good. The change of typography did nothing, and the rest of the page suddenly gleamed with a terrible whiteness.

It was a headline with a catchy idea, but

it led nowhere. The whole ad had to *sell,*
the copy had to sing when you put it all
together, or nobody would read and act on
it. *So what have you been doing the last
twenty-four hours?* Her thoughts had taken
on a brash tone she didn't quite feel, but
hanging fire on the ad copy made her edgy.

Several pieces of discarded copy lay beside her typewriter, and she picked up one
and re-read it.

Nothing happens by accident. Every
effect comes from its prior cause and in
turn becomes the cause of the effect that
follows it. Causation locks the disorderly
flow of life into networks of cause-and-
effect that . . .

Mary Alice dropped the page into the
wastebasket. That was stuff reworked from
her puzzled underlinings in a college philosophy text that somehow hadn't been thrown
out; it barely made sense now, if it ever did.
Spinoza was about as highbrow as you
could get in Philosophy 101B, so she had
tried to tap him for this ad. But it was no
good. What itchy gambler looking for his
luck would read such an ad to the end, much
less grab his checkbook and take a bus to
Atlantic City? She picked up another piece
of copy.

If our world is to make sense at all, we need to know what to expect, to learn the causes of things and to develop reasonable hopes out of our personal experience.

And speaking of experience, a world of pleasure awaits you at 1001 Nights Casino, but I bet you wouldn't eat this baloney if they sliced it with a golden knife . . .

The word *baloney* brought a half smile to her face. The last line had gone out of her head, forgotten in a burst of honesty and anger when she couldn't get the ad copy right. The client wanted something swanky/ritzy like a $2,000 watch or a $100,000 car, but he still weighed 300 pounds and made wet, chirpy sounds when he talked. The idea wasn't working: Spinoza was not upscale, he was off the scale. She was trying an intellectual approach, and nobody gambled for intellectual reasons.

Mary Alice held the wastebasket up to the desk and swept all the bits of paper into it. So much for *that.* She made a new pile of blank sheets beside her typewriter. Upscale . . .

But what did gamblers want, anyhow? To dream they had the golden touch? *Magic?* To feel they'd win even though they knew they wouldn't?

It occurred to Mary Alice that there was a good reason she was stymied on this ad: she had no sympathy with gambling. It was impractical, wasteful, and just plain goofy. If she had any extra money, which she didn't, she would put it in a bank.

A bank . . . now there was a solid idea. Maybe the casino should offer shares in banks instead of merely money. Or maybe golden chips—not the old plastic chips but real silver or gold, with the owner's profile on them. Or Frank Sinatra's. Now *there* was an idea! She jotted it down with a quick tap-tap on the blank page below the Spinoza headline.

However, a minute later the notion left her cold. She leaned forward and put her elbows on the typewriter, her brow against the heel of her hand. This assignment was hopeless. She should zip it back to her boss, Marvin the Knife, before he asked for a progress report. Marvin the Creative Vice President, Marv the Viper, a boss without a creative molecule in his entire brain. His little smile that just bared his teeth suddenly came into her mind, and she turned back to the wastebasket for the trashed pages. Marvin always liked to see the copywriter's notes, no matter how mindlessly boring or off-the-wall they might be, and she had to show him *something*. She tucked the retrieved pages neatly into a folder; perhaps she would write them up as "notes" after lunch.

Mary Alice stood up from her desk and smoothed the front of her skirt, which was feeling a touch snug in the waist, though she knew the skirt's look, as seen from behind, was nice. She was pleasantly round back there, if anyone cared to notice, but she wasn't brazen about it. That morning she had picked out a pastel lemony blouse and an off-white skirt, then knotted a haze-blue kerchief so it fell casually over the open neck of the blouse. The kerchief was folded neatly now in her desk drawer, because she did not like to wear it while working. That would have been too cute.

At the instant she had felt the skirt nip her waist, Mary Alice decided against lunch. She opened the bottom drawer of the desk and took out her jogging shoes; she would walk straight up Fifth Avenue to the Guggenheim and then back, about three and a half miles all told. The exercise and no lunch would take care of her waistline the next time she wore the skirt.

She found a comb in the top drawer and glanced in the mirror on the wall behind her desk. She had hung the mirror there on purpose, opposite the door, where she would see if visitors liked to catch sight of themselves before speaking to her. Marvin always did, at those rare times when he dropped by her office instead of summoning her to his. Sometimes he would talk to her for five minutes, going over a piece of copy line by line, all the while turning his head this way and that, gazing at his face like a prized object that had to be examined from every angle.

I wish I could be like that, she thought, *an ugly stinker who thinks he's beautiful.* However, mirrors held no magic for her, and she stared frankly into this one with her usual candid eye. Her hair looked nice today—more or less. Red hair had a way of being unruly at times, or at least hers did. It was not really red but a muted tone, something between russet and sand, though not exactly sandy, either, which would have driven her crazy. Dark eyelashes, firm eyebrows, and a fresh complexion took away from the redness of her hair, saving her from the bland sandiness that some redheads suffer. Her father was a little like that, fading away at the brows. However, the feature that made people think of her as a real redhead was the brash galaxy of freckles that wheeled across her nose and face. From the moment she had learned to look into mirrors, she had always *liked* her freckles. They were . . . well, different; her feelings were in her face, and the freckles were like crosscurrents of a spirit that splashed and rippled for all to see.

She patted a few straggling strands of hair into place and looked at her lips. They were full and red, and she did not need makeup, which she did not often wear, in any case. The fat client came into her mind; he had been dapper in an unpleasant way, and he had looked at her, pursing his lips, as if she were an upscale treat he might fancy. She would definitely get off the assignment.

At twenty-five, Mary Alice was a typical New Yorker: young, eager, and from out of town. She had gone to a Midwest college for four years and then come to New York after sending off a hundred carefully typed résumés. An entry-level job at a major oil company bored her silly for the better part of a year, but one Friday evening at a party, she heard about a job in an advertising agency; she wrote ads all weekend to give herself a "book," and on Monday after work she went for an interview. The man who saw her was about five years older than herself but already a senior executive; he read her ads, laughed a few times to himself, then hired her on the spot. "Anybody who writes so many lousy ads in forty-eight hours can make it," he said, smiling. "Just write one good one a year, and everybody will think you're a genius."

In the past two years she had worked hard to make a place for herself in the agency and also found time to go out with a few men. Best of all, she had finally lucked into her own apartment.

In fact, Mary Alice had done just about everything she wanted to do in Manhattan except fall in love, which—although both unlikely and predestined—was about to occur on that lovely day in May when she decided to skip lunch in favor of a brisk walk uptown. The story of that fateful noon hour and its aftermath through the rest of the summer and into the fall would squarely prove Spinoza's case, to a degree that might compel even Mary Alice's belief in the idea, if she had known.

So to be perfectly fair about the matter, it was not entirely by chance that she had walked up Fifth Avenue, gone into the Guggenheim Museum, and reached the top of the ramp at the very moment something landed on the roof and shattered the round skylight.

Twenty-five minutes earlier she had started out from her office in midtown Manhattan, to rid herself of an ounce around the middle and an irksome frame of mind. The strenuous pace of the walk had made her feel very good indeed, and as she climbed the spiraling ramp, she still kept up a stride that stretched her calves. She paid scant heed to the current exhibition (all it was worth, actually) and at last found herself out of breath but tasting the air of triumph at the top. And this was the moment at which an event took place, not by accident, that changed her whole life.

Only a few noontime museum wanderers were on hand when the skylight burst inward, sending a glassy shower down the stairwell. Mary Alice shrieked and turned to flee, but a contrary impulse held her there. She stood her ground and covered her face against the spray of broken glass, then peeked between her fingers at a gently rounded silver disk that seemed to have settled on top of the museum like a saucer on top of a bowl. The disk pulsed with a faint orange aura that was beautiful to see. People had scattered, and a security guard fled past her down the ramp making garbled sounds, but somehow Mary Alice's fear had flowed away; she did not want to move. Her hands fell from her face, and she gazed at the shiny metal skin of the object that had just capped the roof of the museum and smashed the shallow glass dome into tinkling slivers.

The Guggenheim is built like the upper half of an ice-cream cone; its circular walls are canted slightly outward from bottom to top, with a continuous ramp winding around the inside. The glassed opening at the top of the cone lets the natural light of day fall amply upon all inside levels of the building's core; but now, with the skylight blocked by a strange object, the museum interior was suddenly cast into ghostly shadows.

Somewhere down below, people were crying and shouting, but from above Mary Alice's head came a sweet whining noise, like a high note on a violin; it seemed to descend from the curved metal surface that now closed the hole in the museum's roof. For an instant she imagined a construction accident or a helicopter crash; but as she watched, a tiny round opening appeared in the metal skin, growing like the lens aperture of a camera. Suddenly a skinny ladder scooted down, touching the ramp ten feet away from her. The opening was dark for a moment, and then a pair of feet in loafers came through, followed by a pair of legs in khaki chinos.

Somebody's making a movie, she thought, *or a television commercial.* But there were no cameras, no director, no bored crew standing around. A man with his back toward her was climbing down the ladder. A thought popped into her head: *I want to talk to him.*

The man wore a white polo shirt and carried a light blue sport jacket draped over one arm. The jacket swayed with his movements, and the ladder looked very flimsy. If it gave way, he would fall straight down the hollow core of the building, where empty space yawned beneath him.

For a second she held her breath, but he

made it down safely. At the bottom he turned, shook out the jacket, and put it on. He was young, with a very pale face, but he possessed the handsomest head of red hair Mary Alice had ever seen. She caught a glint of coppery fuzz on his forearms as he slipped into his jacket; with a tan he might look healthy and likable and not strange at all. Oddly, he rubbed his eyelids, as if he had been sleeping.

Then the redheaded young man gazed directly into her eyes and smiled. "Beautiful," he murmured, and his smile held her for a long second.

A cool tickle went down her spine, as if gentle hands were touching her in impossible places. Something told her she would like this red-haired man.

"Mary Alice," she said, offering her hand.

"4-S-T," he said. He took her hand and shook it, and she felt a warm, pleasant tingle from his dry touch. He had spoken his name so smoothly that Mary Alice heard "Forrest."

"Is that your name?" she asked. "Forrest?"

He seemed not to hear her question but looked at the round museum walls and the ramp, winding in shadow down to ground level. "Do you live here?" he asked. She was too surprised to reply, but just then her

eye caught another young man halfway
down the ladder, and two new faces in the
open hatch. In a moment three more young
men had come down from the silvery thing
on the roof, and each happened to have
the same thick red hair. They could have
been brothers, near the same age. Her
hand went to her own muted red hair, and
she wondered if she looked faded next to
them. Forrest was somehow different from
the other three. It was in the way he stood
casual but poised, the way he looked at
her, and in the openness of his face.

The hubbub down below was dwindling
into silence as people fled the building, but
now Mary Alice noticed two guards moving
hesitantly up the ramp. They were plainly
not in a hurry, and they sidled close to the
wall. She could see them at the point at
which they came opposite to where she was
standing, but then they passed out of sight
as they moved to the side underneath her.
One held a walkie-talkie into which he
spoke now and then, reporting to someone
not in view. The two were just now rounding
the second level, whispering nervously to
each other.

She was not sure she should be getting
into this, but she pointed to the guards and
spoke in a low voice. "They'll stop you,"
she said.

Forrest looked at her, then at the guards.

They had their hands on their holsters, and Mary Alice caught a jittery menace in their movements. For a moment Forrest seemed to think about something, then he turned to his three friends and put out his left hand; the others all reached out hands to touch his. He took a pencil from his breast pocket and pointed the eraser end toward the silver object still blocking the skylight. Something happened to Mary Alice's vision then, but by squeezing her eyelids near shut she saw the metal of a . . . craft?—was that what it was?—shimmer and fade into clear blue sky.

Suddenly her scalp ached. Electric force pulled the hair straight up from her head, and a blind impulse to flee rushed up inside. But somehow she fought back the fear. Everything in the last few minutes had come so fast . . . what was happening here? She grasped the central fact that there was no time now to look for explanations. She could only react, and her clearest instinct was that Forrest, whoever he was, needed a friend. And she wanted to be that friend. Even if she didn't know it yet, there *had* to be an explanation for the crash, for the vanishing . . . spacecraft?

Was that it? An experimental plane, maybe? Were these young men with the Air Force? No uniforms?

It didn't matter: the practical thing right

now was not to hold back but to get out quick. But still she wondered: what *had* happened? Above, the skylight gaped empty and blue, and glass sparkled underfoot. That much was real. She caught the sound of the guards scuffing through shards of debris as they drew nearer. Now she really had to do something.

"Don't worry," Mary Alice said. "We'll walk down together. Just act like you belong here."

Beyond her impulse to get to know this young man named Forrest, she had no reason to intervene, but she took the lead and the others followed down the ramp. Mary Alice noticed one of them looking at the paintings. "I don't know anything about art," he said, "but this is . . ." He fell silent for some reason, and the others smiled.

In a moment the guards came into sight. Forrest waved to them and they froze. The one with the walkie-talkie dropped it. Mary Alice said, "Leave this to me." She recognized one of the guards—he had run yelling past her a few minutes earlier—and she walked straight up to him. She motioned toward the skylight opening and said, "You people have a lot of explaining to do."

"Hold it lady," the guard said. "What's your name?" He was a shifty-eyed man with a shiny bald head and a harsh voice. He had lost his cap running down the ramp.

"Who are these guys? I didn't see them here before."

"I'm not surprised," she said. Her voice had a sharp edge. "You were too busy running away. I was here when the roof fell in, and they're my cousins, and if you say one more word, you'll hear from my lawyer."

She said it as though she meant it, even though she didn't know a lawyer. The guards stood stiffly for a moment, undecided. Forrest eyed them carefully, and they suddenly looked confused.

"We can go now," Forrest said, and Mary Alice and her new friends strolled past the guards, who made no move to stop them but stood looking on, as if puzzled by their own actions.

Forrest touched Mary Alice's elbow as they continued down the ramp. "You come with me," he said. "We have to get through the crowd." Outside on the sidewalk, people clustered to look into the museum. Just inside the street exit, Forrest said to the other three young men, "Keep in touch—okay?" They shook hands awkwardly, then the three others pushed out into the crowd and were lost to Mary Alice's sight, though she had the distinct impression they were headed in different directions.

Forrest took her arm and said, "Okay, here goes," and they went out through the door. A man said, "What happened?" as they pushed past him, but Forrest shook his head and shrugged. He said over his shoulder, "Something fell on the skylight, but they're fixing it." He put his arm around Mary Alice and guided her with him through the crowd, first to the other side of Fifth Avenue and then into Central Park. By the time they got to the park, he was simply resting his arm on her shoulders like an old friend. It felt nice, but she moved to put a little distance between them now that they were away from the throng.

Forrest glanced up to the sky; he blinked and shielded his eyes for a moment against the brightness of the late spring sun. She liked the casual way he walked, and as they strolled, he took off his jacket and carried it slung over his shoulder. "I can't get over all this green," he said, looking at the trees bursting with new foliage. In open daylight he was really pale, but his red hair took on the color of rusty iron, not glittering in the sun.

Acting on her instincts had worked fine, but Mary Alice had gone long enough without asking questions. Now she had to find out who Forrest was and where he came from. She had done him a big favor back at the museum. It was partly out of a generous impulse, even if she did want to get to know him; but now, just who had she done the favor for? And what had happened? Where did he come from? What was he doing here? Would she ever see him again? No, that wasn't the question, but why had he smiled at her so warmly, and why did she feel so nice when he smiled?

Well, she needed to know. Lots of men smiled and meant nothing at all, but somehow this redheaded man's face looked natural and unaffected. And his eyes were unusual, a deeper shade of blue, not azure, but dark solid blue, almost a grayish purple. He was young, and yet his eyes seemed oddly serious and unyouthful. A thought came into her head: *He's from Mars—and that was his ship.*

Abruptly she said, "I think I should tell someone about you. . . ."

"What would you tell them?" he asked lightly. In fact, he did not look concerned at all, and his question was reasonable. Who would believe her if she told the truth about what she had seen in the museum? But she said, "Where are you from and how did you get here?"

Forrest gazed at her. He seemed to be thinking of a reply, and his eyes changed color a little, growing a shade darker. At last his face cleared and he said, "You *saw* how I got here. It was a slight miscalculation—we meant to land a few seconds earlier over here in the park. And where am I from?'' He looked up into the empty blue sky and pointed toward the west. ''Look there tonight.''

He gazed at her again, and again the thought came into her head: *Mars.* She believed it, and she didn't believe it; she had always trusted her first answers to questions, even if they went against common sense. Red-haired or not, Forrest could be an ordinary American male. He had no accent, and he wore clothes you could buy anywhere. There had to be a better explanation for everything that had happened, something closer to normal.

''I don't believe you,'' she said, shaking her head. She didn't mean the words to come out so stiffly, because they did not quite represent what she was feeling.

''And I don't believe you,'' he said, again with a smile that she liked and wanted to trust. ''I don't believe you think I'm lying. The truth is, you don't know what to believe.''

She started to protest, but he was right. Still and all, it didn't make sense that she should be here, strolling through the park with someone who had dropped out of the sky and then taken up with her like a casual friend. What a way to spend her lunch hour! She looked at her wristwatch and was shocked to see the time. ''Oh, hell,'' she said, almost to herself. She was going to be late for a meeting that Marvin had scheduled right after lunch. He liked to make sure no one was playing games on company time.

"You have something important to do?"

"You bet," Mary Alice said. "My job!" This crazy excursion had gone far enough; she had to get back to a very real job at Schuyler & Blitz, Fifth Avenue and Fifty-third Street, New York City, on the planet Earth. That was real, it was necessary, and it was what she *would* do.

"Let me help you," Forrest said. "Just look into my eyes and think of where you want to be." It was silly, but she looked. His eyes were really nice to look at; they were turning a rich purplish gray, and they seemed to dance. He was charming, no doubt about it, but Mary Alice had to get back to her office. However, she could not help imagining that the purple depths of his eyes were like the deep open sky of a planet where a pitifully thin atmosphere never deflected or absorbed the harsher rays of the sun or masked the darkness of space. . . . *But what am I doing here?*

It was enough. Mary Alice turned to leave the park. But they were no longer in the park; they stood on the sidewalk in front of her office building.

Her scalp prickled with a chill that shot through her body, even though she felt the warm sun on the back of her neck. What on earth was happening with this man? Had he hypnotized her? She shivered with a crazy coldness she could not control, but she looked at her watch again and saw that she still had two minutes to get upstairs for the meeting. The meeting. Routine, everyday reality was very good. She had to hold on to it.

"I don't know how you did that," she said, not looking into his eyes now. "But thank you . . . I guess."

"Meet me after work—right here—and I'll tell you how," Forrest said.

Mary Alice turned away without replying. She was off-balance and dizzy and simply had to get away from this person and back to surroundings she could trust.

Not that *trust* was the right word for the reality that faced her in the meeting a few minutes later. She was the last to arrive, and two of the other copywriters were already droop-faced with cigarettes, a sure sign they were nervous, fearful, and quietly angry. Marvin sat at the head of the table and tapped a pencil on an unused ashtray, a mannerism that he would not have tolerated in anyone else.

"Thank you for joining us," he said, smiling. It was amazing how ugly his smile could be. The digital clock on the conference-room wall showed Mary Alice she was only a minute late, and she ignored his greeting. Marvin could not expect an apology for the minute, and she would also ignore his little smile. She took her seat, determined that no look of guilt or obedience would cross her face.

Marvin put down the pencil carefully, spread his hands palm down on the blond oak table, looked at each person in turn, and cleared his throat. "In case any of you were planning to take the afternoon off," he said, *"don't.* We are having a crisis. Al''—Al was the senior vice-president in charge of the Sunrise Cola account— "should be here any minute. He will tell us that our client is disgusted with our advertising." Marvin was establishing the fact that the copywriters in this room were at fault. And at risk. He looked once more around the table; the narrow, windowless room seemed to have grown very stuffy in the last minute. "Unless . . ." He spoke in a mild voice and did not have to finish his sentence. Everyone knew what he meant: *Unless* they came up with a new campaign that the client liked.

"I don't blame Al for being upset. Sunrise is a twenty-million-dollar account. That's three million dollars in commissions. Approximately this agency's yearly rent for four floors of a nice building. One hundred thousand square feet. A nice place for you to work. However, I do blame the client for having a soft drink that tastes like a hospital's bathwater, but since we can do nothing about *that,* I also blame you for not disguising this unfortunate fact. And I blame myself for being too nice." Marvin smiled a very wide smile, the smile that everyone called his alligator smile. He was being candid and taking them into his confidence. "I will not be nice anymore," he said, looking directly at Mary Alice. "Well?"

He paused, and a stricken silence fell over the room, a silence broken only by the soulless buzz and click of the digital clock as it turned a minute. Mary Alice wished someone would speak. He was right about the product, of course. It tasted like soapy lemonade. *Maybe a little bird lands in a grove of lemon trees and—*

"Hello?" Marvin called out, as if he were in the doorway of a house that might be empty. "Anybody home?"

Twenty minutes later the room was full of smoke, but the meeting was still void of ideas. Eight had been proposed, just kickoff notions, as someone said nervously, to get the game rolling; but none of the eight took the deadly smile from Marvin's face for even a second. Mary Alice wondered how long he could keep it up. It must be a strain

to smile ugly for so long, but she remembered reading somewhere that smiling takes
fewer muscles than frowning. Marvin was a
lazy and talentless man. Correction. He
knew how to live off other people's ideas
and had a talent for putting a verbal knife
to your throat.

Her pad was full of doodles and notes of
the silly ideas everyone else had offered,
but her mind stayed blank. Marvin looked in
her direction now and then; she was the
only one who had not spoken. She was also
the youngest person in the room, but she
tended to come up with a greater flow of
ideas than the others. However, it wasn't
happening right now when she needed it.
The bird in the lemon grove was not worth
mentioning. She was afraid Marvin would
ask, "Out to lunch?" with that smile of his,
the way he sometimes did when a copywriter was silent in a meeting. She made a
long, empty oval on her pad as if she were
sketching an idea, and she kept her eyes on
the oval, wondering what to do next.

Al suddenly appeared in the open doorway. He was an older man, very tall, and he
usually wore a loose tweed suit, a carefully
tailored shirt, and an earth-tone wool neck-
tie. He had an easy manner that made him
seem calm at all times, and the first thing he
always did when he came into a room for
a meeting was to fumble around for his pipe

and find it, with a look of surprise and pleasure, in the third pocket he searched.

"Sorry I'm late, Marv," he said. He
waved his hand in a way that might have
been a greeting to everyone in the room, or
an apology. He slumped casually into a
seat at the foot of the table. "Caught in
traffic. Something crazy happened uptown,
dunno what, but there was traffic all the way
down." He nodded pleasantly but vaguely
to everyone at the table, but his eyes wid-
ened when he noticed Mary Alice.

"Hey! I don't get it," he said, looking at
her. "I saw you uptown in the park. How the
devil did you get down here ahead of me?
I was in a taxi already, and you were walking along with some guy." He seemed baf-
fled but in a nice way.

"In the park?" Mary Alice said, playing
for time. She did not want to lie, but how
could she tell the truth? And did she know
the truth? She still couldn't say what had
actually happened, but dodging the question made her feel guilty, because she liked
Al.

"Funny," Al said, stuffing his pipe. "I
could swear you were strolling along with a
young redheaded fellow while I was hung
up in traffic. At Eighty-ninth Street. Twenty
minutes ago. I guess you flew," he said with
a nice smile that dropped the subject.

Al was the kind of boss who put everyone

at ease when there was a crisis, and maybe it was just an act, but it worked. His manner was exactly what the meeting needed, and Mary Alice felt herself relax; she breathed easier even though she had no ideas. Marvin usually became a little more neutral when Al was in the room.

In the pressure of the meeting, she had lost sight of the paradox of Forrest. He had begun to seem imaginary, but now Al's questions brought her back to the puzzle of who Forrest was and what had happened. If the problem at the museum caused a traffic jam and Al was caught in it, that was real. So a spaceship, or something, *had* landed on the museum.

Mary Alice looked at the long empty oval on her yellow pad and saw that it might be a saucer seen from an angle, and she put portholes on it and said, "Marvin, how about this?" She did not look at him for a reaction but continued to talk about her sudden idea.

As she spoke, she drew a high school with students pouring into it. Early morning. This particular client always wanted to reach a younger market—adults wouldn't touch his cola. Inside the school, before class, the kids had gathered around a soft drink machine, and mingling with the kids, she drew three or four little green men. The kids were buying Sunrise Cola and punching each other on the arm and saying, "Gotcha!" and "Wake up, Charlie!", but they paid no attention to the little green men, who were also buying the cola. The men were not drinking it—they were loading the bottles into a futuristic-looking wheelbarrow that floated just above the floor. One of the kids punched a little green man on the arm by mistake, and the punch made a musical *bing!* sound and the action froze on-screen.

"I'm going for a science-fiction kind of background, Marvin, but setting it here on Earth. You can see these little green men at the Coke machine—sorry, Al, I didn't mean to call it that—and they're loading up with Sunrise, and the kids are just treating them like they're other kids—normal, you know? And you see a flying saucer hovering outside the school, but no one's noticed it yet?" She paused and looked up.

"That's off-the-wall, Mary Alice," Marvin said, wrinkling his nose but still smiling somehow. "Anybody else?"

Al leaned forward, slipped out of his tweed jacket, and hung it on the back of the chair next to him. He took the pipe from between clenched teeth and spoke. "Not so fast, Marv, hold your horses, I like it." He looked at Mary Alice with a hopeful expression on his face. "You got great visuals. I know old Roger like the back of my hand.

I can sell him the school scene and maybe the flying saucer.''

''But, Christ, it'll cost half a million,'' Marvin said. ''Think about the special effects.'' His smile had suddenly gone away.

''Don't worry, Marv,'' Al said calmly. ''We get fifteen percent on top of every dollar we spend, and if Roger likes it, he *likes* it.'' He turned back to Mary Alice and said, ''But what's the payoff? What's the pitch? What's the headline?''

Mary Alice focused carefully on Al, but she felt everyone at the table turning toward her. Al was much better than Marvin at putting a person on the spot in a productive way, because Al made you like him first. But right now she was not sure of anything except that she had to take an awful chance. '' 'When Your Thirst Is Out of This World'?'' she asked, wishing she could hide.

Al did not nod, but his brown eyes retreated to distant shores of thought, and he slowly found his mouth with his pipe. He was not looking at anything in the room, only at some inner scene that no one else could see. He leaned back in his chair, tilting the front legs off the floor, still with his faraway look. For Mary Alice time stood still, despite the robot buzz-click of the digital clock; the only other sound in the room was a string of little sucking pops as Al drew air through a balky pipe. Marvin's careful fist made tiny quiet notes on his yellow pad, but he did not dare interrupt Al's mental operations, whatever they were.

At last Al brought his tilted chair back level and knocked the dottle from his pipe and stuck it stem downward in the breast pocket of the brown tweed jacket hanging on the chair. He spoke. "Do a storyboard, Marvin. My office, ten o'clock tomorrow." He grinned at Mary Alice and stood up to leave, gathering his jacket casually from the back of the chair. "Thank you, young lady. This has been a good meeting. I knew I could count on this group." The way he came out with the word *group* was rich and wonderful. It included everybody, but it left Mary Alice feeling that he really meant *her*. "Marv's always telling me how good his group is, and he's right."

Al nodded to the room at large and sauntered out, but he turned and popped his head in the doorway again. "Say, Marv," he said. "Think of two more just as good. I like to go in with three storyboards, you know. Give the dumb prick a choice."

Mary Alice blazed away at her typewriter. She wrote a campaign in which Count Dracula was foiled by a *shpritz* of Sunrise Cola—at sunrise, of course—and then she wrote two more. Marvin appeared at her door around four o'clock and looked at himself in her mirror, but she waved him away. She was not about to give him anything until the last minute. Let him wait, let him suffer. She went back to the Dracula campaign and described Dracula in a way that made him seem like Marvin. She had him preening in a mirror even though she knew vampires had no reflections. *But they do at Schuyler & Blitz,* she thought.

Finally, at a quarter to six, she went to Marvin's office with four campaigns, all quite clever, if she did say so herself. He looked them over, picked the Dracula campaign, and put the rest in his drawer. He showed her a dull idea of his own that he had already started to turn into a storyboard, so she knew that two of the three ideas presented to Al would be hers.

Now her part was done; Marvin would work with the layout artist to turn the copy into a series of sketches that told the ad's story like a cartoon strip, which was what Al needed tomorrow. Marvin never let anyone except himself make a presentation of finished storyboards to Al, even if he had to work all night, and when she volunteered to stay overtime and help, he said no thanks.

Mary Alice walked back to her office, covered her typewriter, and straightened her desktop. It had been a really good afternoon's work. No. Most copywriters would not have been able to write so much usable copy in a week, and Marvin not in his entire lifetime. She wrote easily when ideas flowed, and that was most of the time. If she were at cross-purposes with the writing or with herself, then she got stuck. Getting stuck was a symptom of a problem which a mere rearrangement of words would not fix. At that point she usually had to stop and look at herself, though not in a mirror.

Her best habit, as she saw it, was to look back at what she was feeling and figure out why. You had to pause to let your understanding catch up. There were lots of ways to feel good, but only one way she had found to cope with distress. From an early age she had tried to treat every pain—whether it was anger, disappointment, jealousy, fear, or whatever—as if it had a value and an importance; it was never made light of in her heart of hearts. Pain slighted was pain remembered—even if it was forgotten. So habitually she gave every bad feeling its due, and especially every numbness of spirit.

This had been her rule, ever since she was a little girl with a mother who cared how she felt, that nothing that made her sad was to be overlooked, that no sorrow was negligible. And from experience she knew that if she felt a disappointment keenly enough at the moment it happened, without glossing it over or denying it, and in a parallel way found some of its ramifications within herself, then it would gradually pass. Controlling emotions by minimizing them or cutting them off from full expression could become a dangerous habit; it was turning away from yourself and pretending to be someone you weren't. You could also fall into a pattern of not trying to do something difficult because you feared, often unconsciously, that you would fail and thus have a bad feeling about yourself that you couldn't cope with. But Mary Alice had felt really wonderful with Al's acceptance of her idea in the meeting, and so worked well the rest of the afternoon. She had taken a chance and won.

Well, she had done the job, and now it was time to go. The day was still lovely, and a long spring twilight would be just starting, and she could take a roundabout way home. She could walk over to the East River at Beekman Place and then back to Third Avenue and downtown a few blocks to her apartment in Murray Hill. Maybe she would do the laundry and read a book, and then a long bath and more of the book at bedtime. Not much of an evening for a young woman in her mid-twenties in Manhattan, but Mary Alice was still enjoying the fresh possession of a new apartment where she could do whatever she pleased. There would be plenty of time to do other things later on.

Mary Alice left her office door open, took a last quick glance at herself in the mirror, and walked down the hall. After six the offices were mostly empty; the cleaning crew came in two hours later, and there was a sad atmosphere in the interim period when the whole floor seemed devoid of life, no matter who remained. She did not like to stay late, after the pulse of the business day had come to a stop.

When she came out of the elevator on the ground floor, the lobby still bustled with people leaving the building, but a blue-suited security guard stood beside the night desk near the revolving door that opened onto Fifth Avenue. As she started through the door, a voice behind her said, "Hey! Wait!" The urgent tone made her pause and turn.

Forrest was coming across the lobby toward her. She had forgotten his offer to meet her. Maybe she was still not quite sure that everything that had happened was real. *No, I didn't want the disappointment if he wasn't there.* Well, now she didn't have to avoid the disappointment anymore.

"I'm sorry I'm late," she said as he came up to her, though she was not feeling sorry at all. He had startled her, but now a sudden little curl of pleasure made itself felt, like an invisible threat floating and winding itself around inside her. "I had to work late," she said. "How about supper?" He smiled and nodded, and his bush of hair seemed redder than she recalled.

At Burger Heaven, Forrest's first meal on Earth was a hamburger, which he clearly loved, but what really seemed to impress him was water. He kept having his glass refilled, and drinking it down.

"I can't get over this. . . . All I want," he said after his third glass. He had told her, matter-of-factly, where he was from, but she was not ready to accept it. She had made up her mind to ask him anything and everything that came into her head, to listen to him and to reserve judgment; she had no particular goal. She just wanted to hear what he would say, and he said a great deal. For good reason, water was exciting to him: only nine springs or wells were left on his home planet, and their flow, which surfaced in carefully guarded caves, was monitored constantly. He also talked of the hopelessly thin atmosphere, and the blue and yellow clouds that made the noonday sky as colorful as an Earth sunset; and the red-powder deserts with their broken and abandoned canal systems, and the oxygen vines that grew near every cave entrance, without which it would be impossible to

breathe. Nobody lived on the surface anymore, but everyone could come up for a
look at the bleak exterior of their world and
go back down again. Twice she asked him
how many people there were, but somehow
he talked of other things without answering
her. When she pressed him a third time, he
said, "Not many. That's why I'm—we're—
here," and in the face of this answer she felt
suddenly uneasy pursuing that line of conversation.

Since Forrest had no money, Mary Alice
paid for their hamburgers and saw that he
looked at the change-making process very
curiously.

"What do you use for money?" she
asked as she was putting her billfold into her
shoulder bag.

"We don't have any," he said. "Everyone shares." That didn't seem possible, but
then neither was he. She would have to hear
more.

"When it's dark," Forrest said, "I can
show you my home. We can go into the
park."

"That's not a good idea," Mary Alice
said. He looked curiously innocent to her,
but he would find out soon enough about
the dangers of New York. "We'll go back
to my building," she said. "There's a terrace on top, like an observation deck, but
it's not for the public. We can go there."

· · ·

A pale yellow sunset lingered in the western sky for half an hour, and as the paleness darkened, the color of the sky shifted swiftly but by little unseen stages, first to a pastel blue, then to the stealthier blueness of dusk. A kind of haze seemed to hang in the air, but the sky was cloudless, and a lustrous evening star came out well above the horizon, a single dot of silver in the empty stretch of heaven.

"Is that it?" she asked. Forrest shook his head and said, "Wait." A little later he pointed out a smaller clear-shining dot, and Mary Alice could make out a pinkish tinge when she focused on the planet just off the center of her vision. Mars.

"Yes, you can see the color," Forrest said. "The deserts give it a pink shimmer, even so far away."

They stood talking for a while as the sky grew darker. To the south, the shape of the island of Manhattan lay beneath them like the deck of an enormous boat, a ship loaded with a glittering cargo of lights, ready to sail out onto a night sea. The sky had never seemed so vast to Mary Alice, nor Manhattan so beautiful. Forrest gazed at the carpeting of lights and murmured, *"Alioiia . . ."*

"What . . . ?" Mary Alice said.

"Alioiia—they're phosphorescent flow-

ers, tiny and very precious." A handful of
flowers, he told her, grew in every room
and were watered once a year. They gave
off a kind of twilight but took scarcely any
energy. The flowers were rare now; they
had been slowly disappearing in the last ten
thousand years. Forrest had been speaking
of time spans that she could not compre-
hend, speaking almost as if he remembered
such times, and his conversation about the
things and places of another world had a
curious effect on her. Somewhere in the pre-
vious hour she had begun to believe him, to
believe what he was saying; and if her belief was not very strong, at least she was
convinced he was not lying. The events a
few hours earlier at the museum were so
extraordinary and had happened so fast
that she could not be sure what she had
seen. Forrest explained how he had taken
her from the park to her office building by
means of a time-stop ability that he could
manage over short distances—an ability his
people had developed as a way of escaping from danger. It sounded plausible,
though she could not follow his explanation
that if you compressed an object to make it
incredibly small, time would stop and the
object would turn into light.

The fact was, he had begun to hold her
attention with his stories of life on Mars,
though it also helped that she had liked him

to begin with. Her last inner barrier melted
when she heard Forrest's tale of the sandbears, the shy little creatures who lived in
the desert and were smaller than mice.

"Sometime I'll draw you a picture of
one," Forrest said. "You'd love to see him,
but he couldn't live here on Earth. He's
about so big"—Forrest indicated two inches with his thumb and forefinger—"with
fuzzy white-and-pink fur and tiny blue eyes.
He's very friendly and once in a while goes
to sleep clinging to your hair, and when he
does that, you have to be very careful not
to hurt him. We have lots of stories—I guess
you would call them children's stories—
about sandbears."

Mary Alice said, "Tell me one of those,"
and so he told her a story about a young
sandbear who came out of his cave on the
banks of the canal one day and found himself wondering why the sand was red and
why the canal was dry. He lived alone,
because all sandbears live alone most of
the time except when they give birth—actually, they sprout, since there's only one sex,
and when their time comes, they root themselves in the earth, like plants.

At this point Mary Alice broke in, "Plants
here on Earth can have a sex difference
too."

"Really? Amazing," Forrest said, and
went on with his story, telling how the baby

grows from the sandbear's navel. At first he is a bud not even as big as a match head, but he stays with his parent for a year until he has grown large enough to forage for himself and find the microscopic desert plants that sandbears live on. This particular bear wandered away from his cave while he was thinking about things he didn't understand, and a cold winter sandstorm made him lose his way. The bear was so young and inexperienced that he did not realize he was almost ready to sprout. When he felt the tickling of life at his navel and the cold wind whipped around his stubby ears, he had to dig his feet into the sand in a hurry and hold on fast to keep the bud-baby from being blown away.

He was frightened, and he tried to make himself small and snug so that the wind could not budge him. But at last the bud broke free, and a bitter gust of wind caught the tiny newborn bear and rolled it across the desert. The parent bear tore himself loose from his root-place and ran leaping after his child. He pounced on it just as it was about to sail over a cliff into a deep canyon. He scooped up the baby but could not stop himself from flying away in the wind, which carried him high in the air over the canyon. Then an updraft whirled the sandbear even higher, still clutching the baby; and they rose, tumbling over and over, far above the sandstorm and into the freezing upper atmosphere of Mars.

Below, the sandbear caught sight of the endless, wavering figure of a ribbonbird, a creature a thousand miles long but so light and airy that the slightest breeze would send it soaring. In fact, ribbonbirds spent their entire lives fluttering through the atmosphere of Mars, sometimes trailing one end down to the desert floor but never coming to rest. As he fell, the sandbear managed to grasp one edge of the ribbonbird's flat body and pull himself onto it. The turbulence of the storm whipped the long ribbon up and down abruptly, but the bear held on. As small as he was, he still weighed enough to lower a mile of the bird's body, and when the storm at last blew itself out, he came trailing down softly to the red sandy surface of the desert. By chance, the storm had tossed and held him in the air all the way around the planet and brought him home again, baby and all, not half a *siiew* (about a mile) from his cave.

As the sandbear climbed the cliff wall above the canal and made his way into his cozy cave nest, it suddenly occurred to him that he had not yet named his child. Here he was, carrying this tiny creature, once again warmly attached to his navel and only three days old, for they had spent that long a time in the air, and the sandbear thought,

What shall I call him? And after a while it came into his mind to name him *Wonder,* because the dangers around the child's birth had come about when the sandbear was not paying attention to himself but wondering why the sand was red and the canal dry.

Forrest fell silent at the end of the tale. It had been beautiful, and she wanted it to go on, but now the air on the observation deck of the building had grown chill in the few minutes it took to tell the story. Overhead, the sky was darker but now beginning to be crowded with stars, and a breeze had sprung up from the north. Mary Alice put her arms into the sweater she had been carrying over her shoulders and pulled the garment close around her. She looked soberly at Forrest. Where would he sleep tonight? Had he even thought about it? The question had not come into her mind until this moment.

"I guess you don't have a place to stay," she said. He had not moved since finishing the story, and his face was profiled against the Jersey skyline. She did not want the evening to end just yet.

"Would they let me stay here?" he asked, turning to look at the bench on the upper level of the observation deck. "I'm used to much colder weather. This is like a hot day. . . ." He was hesitant, as if he knew how odd it would sound. "At home," he said.

Mary Alice shook her head. "No, you can't stay here. I have a couch you can use tonight, and we'll talk about what you do tomorrow."

At her apartment, which was a studio with a nice view of the East River on the eighteenth floor of an old building in Murray Hill, Forrest looked on as Mary Alice made the couch into a bed. With extra sheets and a pillow from the closet, it would be comfortable—she glanced to gauge Forrest's height—if he kept his knees flexed. But no, that wouldn't do. He should take her bed in the sleeping alcove, and she would fit on the couch very easily. She had slept there for several nights before the bed was delivered, and it was fine.

"This is for me," she said. "You'll sleep over there." She pointed to the alcove. Her voice carried far more assurance than she felt. Having a man overnight—one she couldn't possibly know, even if she liked him—gave her doubts that she firmly put down.

Forrest started to object, but she said, "Don't argue. This is my place and you're a guest." Looking at him again, she noticed that during the day he had become quite tan. It was almost a miracle. His hands were as brown as if he had worked outdoors for a month, and the smooth, bronzed skin of his face was very handsome against his red hair.

"Would you like a cup of tea?" she asked. He did not seem to know what tea was, but she explained and he nodded. He spoke the language well enough, but she sensed many gaps that he wanted filled. Mary Alice set the tea things on the small dining table under the window that looked out over the East River, and they sat facing so both could see it. Again, the presence of so much water seemed to bewitch him. He held the cup in his hand, lost in wonder at the powerful glittering surface of the river. The cups were Mary Alice's best, a present from her grandmother, and they were of an odd mold, with a slightly flared rim whose snug contour felt pleasant against one's mouth.

At last Forrest lifted the cup carefully to his lips, as if to test it, then took a sip of tea, which he had cooled with a sizable dollop of milk. He smiled as he lowered the cup from his mouth. "That's nice," he said, running his finger around the rim of the cup. "Very friendly to the lip."

The words startled Mary Alice. Forrest seemed often naïve, yet he was original too. And she suddenly understood something else even more startling: Anyone who could come up with a phrase like "friendly to the lip" could learn to be a copywriter with a little help, could function in her office, could do well in meetings, could play Marvin's game.

"That's very good," she said. "Very good about the cup. It's odd that you have ideas like that. But what would you say about the tea?" He looked blank for a second. "That stuff you're drinking," she said.

"The tea?" He picked up the cup and sipped again. "It will never replace water—there's nothing like water—but this gives me a lift I won't forget."

That was good too. Mary Alice got up and went to her desk for a steno pad. Back at the table, she sat down and said, "Yes? What else?"

In ten minutes she had three ideas for tea ads, all good possibilities, and the agency didn't even have a tea account. Maybe Sunrise Cola could adapt the ideas. If Forrest could toss off new notions so easily . . . but wait—why was she thinking all this? She wondered for a moment but drew a blank and shrugged. It didn't seem to matter. The only thing that mattered was that she could solve Forrest's problem; she would help him put together a book of original ad copy and run him through Personnel, then introduce him to Marvin and Al.

It would be a snap to give him a background; Personnel never checked it out, anyhow. And Al liked to meet young writers, even those with no experience. "We can always use a fresh brain," Al liked to say. "I'll never let this agency suffer from tired brains."

She told Forrest what she wanted to do, and he looked puzzled.

"What's advertising?" he asked.

"Words and ideas and pictures that make people feel they want to buy something."

"What is 'buy'?"

Mary Alice felt her impatience rising. "To exchange money for something—clothes or a car. You remember the hamburger we had earlier? I had to buy it."

"So the purpose of advertising is to get money?"

"To get people to let go of their money," Mary Alice said. "And also for *you* to get money. You need a job."

"A job?"

"Never mind, I'll explain later. First, can you type?"

"Type?"

She took a deep breath and went to her desk, motioning him to follow her. At the desk she uncovered her typewriter and showed it to him, along with an old typing exercise that she sometimes used when she was stuck. He glanced at the exercise and put it aside, then sat down and stared at the keyboard of her portable for a full minute. He closed his eyes as if he were imagining something and wanted no distraction, then opened them again. He put his fingers on the keys and rattled off, "The quick brown fox jumped over the lazy dog." There were no mistakes; the sentence was perfectly typed.

He looked up at Mary Alice. "What does this sentence mean?" he said.

"Nothing. It's just a test sentence that uses all the letters of the alphabet."

"Not quite," he said. "There's no s—but you can fix that, just change *jumped* to *jumps.*" He typed the sentence again. "And it's funny," he said. "This gives me an idea for an ad."

Earlier in the evening they had walked past a store window with a display of word processors, and she had explained the difference between them and typewriters, though she hadn't explained just what it was to type. Now Forrest typed neatly and precisely, drafting copy for a word processor ad using the "quick brown fox" sentence as a headline. The "quick brown fox" was the new word processor, and the "lazy dog" was the old machine that had to be replaced.

"I think you've got the idea now," Mary

Alice said. "But how did you learn to type so fast, just like that?"

"Reflexes . . ." He smiled and opened and closed his fists. "My fingers understood."

"Oh, I see," she said, though she really didn't. Anyhow, it was not important. What mattered was that he could type like a whiz and write better ads quicker than anyone she had ever seen. "We'll do more in the morning," she said, turning off the desk lamp.

Suddenly a thought struck her. He needed a Social Security number, something from Immigration . . . my God, how could she possibly get him a job? He saw the distress in her face and asked what was the matter. She told him in as much detail as she could. Forrest looked thoughtful for a moment, then closed his eyes. He opened them again in a few seconds and grinned. "Don't worry," he said. "I can take care of that."

When she came out of the bathroom, Forrest was already in bed. She turned off the lights, then slipped under the sheets on the couch and fluffed the pillow. It was a cool night, and her pajamas snugged her legs like ski pants.

"Don't you want to use the bathroom?" she said into the darkness.

"Not yet," Forrest's voice came back. "We don't go so often. More economical, I guess."

"How often?" She couldn't believe she was saying this.

"Oh . . ." The hesitancy came back into his voice. "Every third year."

"Forrest, if you can hold it for three years, then you're really a Martian."

"Oh, I am. But it's nothing special. We use up a lot more energy than you do."

"How?" She hadn't seen him exerting himself at all.

"Thinking."

"You'd better not say it that way to anyone else."

"Oh?"

"People might think you were stuck-up."

"Stuck-up?"

"Conceited, vain."

She thought for a moment. "We're not going to tell anybody where you're from, by the way."

"No . . ." He paused. "I didn't think so."

Mary Alice was sleepy, but it felt nice to chat with him across the room in the friendly darkness of her apartment, his voice coming back to her softer than sand . . . like silky sand sifting through her fingers, sand so soft that it flowed like water. . . .

She was just dozing off when a thought brought her awake. What did he expect of her? Martians must have ways of behaving in a social situation, or a personal context, like everybody else. Why not find out?

"I'm not sure how to behave with you," she said. The fresh night air was making her drowsy, and she yawned. He had not answered, so she said, "I don't know what you expect."

"How so?" His voice was now not so soft, and he did not sound sleepy. Maybe Martians didn't have to sleep, either.

"Well, I mean—everything."

"Oh, just do whatever comes into your mind. It's your world—your home."

That sounded reasonable enough, and with the darkness blurring the walls and with the windows opening out into a clear night, Mary Alice lay untroubled on her modest couch, feeling oddly free and at ease. A breeze blew through the apartment, and an image came to her of a huge tree with a nest swaying gently on a high branch. It was a peaceful feeling—as if she were almost alone, even though he was there on the other side of the room. The apartment was small, but since Forrest didn't have to use the bathroom, it was as if she had the place almost to herself. A funny thought occurred to her: she imagined saying, "It's nice you didn't make a pass at me tonight," and he would say, "What's a pass?" and she would laugh and touch his beautiful red hair.

Yes, Forrest was somehow naïve, but he knew enough not to crowd her in any way. Mary Alice turned onto her side to face the window and drift off to sleep. She shifted her head on the pillow until she found just the right spot, and the last thing she remembered was hearing him say, "I'm the one who has to figure out how to behave."

The next morning Mary Alice left Forrest at the typewriter, working on his book of sample ads. He came to her office at lunchtime, and she went over his copy book. Most of his work was very near the mark, but he needed more samples, which he wrote that afternoon and in the evening when she was home again. She corrected and he retyped until almost midnight, but by the next morning he was ready for his interview with Personnel; only a day later Marvin hired him to start the following Monday. From somewhere Forrest had a Social Security card.

Once the process had begun, Mary Alice could not very well ask Forrest to leave her apartment—he was much too close to getting a job, and she couldn't throw him out on the street. She had rescued him after a fashion, and she was to that degree responsible for him—so he stayed at her place, sleeping every night on the bed while she slept on the couch. She realized she was interested in him, but she was not about to let him know. He *looked* normal, but what if Martians were really different—like the sandbears? The distance in their relation had begun to annoy her mildly, but the hiring changed everything. If he wasn't for real in the way she wanted him to be, then he was *in* the way. And if his presence intruded on her life, he *would* have to move, move out at once.

On the day he was hired, they went out to celebrate at her favorite neighborhood restaurant, and when they walked home that evening, in high spirits from having drunk almost enough Beaujolais with dinner, she wished suddenly they could go somewhere else—away together. Forrest had offered to repay her when he got his first check, and for a second or two she was pleased by this; but then somehow she resented it and said, "Save your money."

A gusty breeze ruffled her hair as they walked down the gentle slope of Murray Hill toward her apartment building. The sidewalks had almost emptied, and for a moment she felt they were alone in the city. The weather was changing; although summer was almost at hand, the air had grown cooler with a sudden shift of wind. The apartment might be cool tonight, but the notion came to her of how nice it would be to sleep in the mountains, where the night air was really crisp.

But that was silly. They hardly knew each other, and tomorrow was a working day.

Later that night something—she couldn't say what—woke Mary Alice from a happy dream. She felt vaguely uneasy upon waking, but in the dream she had been sitting on her father's lap, and a puppy, an Irish setter, was trying to leap up into *her* lap, and she was laughing and putting a leash over its head. The puppy was finally about to get into her lap and lick her face when she awoke. Her eyes were blurry for a minute or two, but then she saw that the glowing hands of the clock over her desk pointed to three-fifteen. A few hours of sleep had left her languid but restless, or maybe it was the wine with dinner. The familiar outlines of her room were reassuring, and everything lay cool and quiet around her now, so quiet that the faint pulse throbbing in her head seemed ominous. Definitely the wine.

The risen moon hung over the East River, a solitary moon whose fruitless glow came fitfully through the window. The dream had been amazingly vivid, and they were laughing so much that recalling it made her lonely; she wished she could enter into the world of the dream again.

The wind rattled a shade, and she sat up

a moment and peered out the window at a moon besieged by clouds. They raced past, beneath and above the moon, and then a larger cloud covered it fully, a long, roiling mass of gray that caught the reflected lights of the city. The wind gusted, and a distant grumble of thunder warned of an approaching storm front. She shivered under the single sheet that covered her on the couch, but she debated getting up for a blanket. She should have thought of it before. Now she did not want to disturb Forrest, and she listened for some sound from him. Why was he there? Why had she let him come into her life? What did she want with him? The room was silent, except for the wind. Was he still there? Or had he faded away in some manner known only to him?

She could smell the rain in the air now, and she would have to get up anyhow to lower the windows. She peered across the room to the bed in the alcove, but it lay in deep shadow. She untangled her feet from the sheet, stood up, and padded barefoot to the opposite side of the room. Yes, he was there, a solid shape on the far side of the bed. The thunder had drawn closer, and a blaze of lightning turned the room stark white. Forrest's eyes were wide open, his face alert, and he was looking directly at her.

"Are you cold?" he said.

She was almost too startled by his eyes to reply but said "No" in a voice that sounded odd to her. At that moment a pattering of raindrops threatened the open windows. She crossed the room to close the window by the table; the wind was blowing from that direction now. Then she came back again to the window near the bed. She lowered it just as the storm broke, and she stood looking out over the streets and buildings swept by rain; but in moments the rain, dashing against the window, blurred the glass so that the scene was hidden.

Another lightning flash, much closer this time, showed Forrest sitting up in bed, still looking at her. A second later thunder crackled monstrously close at hand. Mary Alice jumped despite herself; the nearness of it had the harshness of a blow and frightened her even though she knew she was safe.

"Am I bothering you?" she said. "Do you want a blanket?" The rampaging rain battered the windows, slashing against the glass.

Forrest did not speak but in reply lifted the bedclothes. Lightning lit up the room again, though at a little distance this time, like shielded torches. Thunder followed more slowly as the storm moved away to the east, but the rain still came down in torrents. Mary Alice started back to the couch but suddenly thought, "Until the storm passes," and slipped under the cover Forrest was holding. He wrapped it around her and lay beside her. The place in the bed felt warm, as if he had just moved from it. She had not slept in this bed for almost a week, but it smelled clean, with a faint trace of the sweetness she detected whenever she came close to Forrest. She was a tiny bit fearful, but after all, it was her own bed. She wondered at herself for being in bed with a strange man, but in a way all men were strange, with a strangeness that drew her on. Especially Forrest. Nevertheless, she shivered when he took her hand and gently held her palm to his lips. She drew the hand away, but it returned almost of its own accord to touch his face and then his incredible hair, which seemed to give back a glint of copper even in the darkness. Fear flowed away, and in its place she found desire.

Forrest moved his arm, and she lay her face on his shoulder, her cheek against his warm skin. His hand rested gently on the curve of her hip.

"Are you afraid?" he said. His voice was warm and near, and she was not afraid but did not reply. He whispered, "I like you very much, Mary Alice." Then, as he touched her cheek and lifted her face and turned fully toward her, she understood at last how much she desired the beautiful weight of his body, at whatever moment it might be hers to possess.

When Mary Alice awoke the next morning, Forrest was still sleeping. Apparently Martians did sleep now and then, and this one had a gentle snore, something close to the purr of a dozing cat. The windows were as she had left them last night, open an inch above the windowsill, but outside she could see the sky bright blue and cloudless. In a minute she would get up and raise the window by the bed and let the fresh air wash over her skin. A little tick of fear came back, but then it went away, and she knew she had no regret. She had wanted to learn everything about Forrest, but she had learned nothing except that he was the one for her. *So far,* she told herself. Now she propped herself up on one elbow and gazed at him naked and helpless, asleep beside her in this still new bed. His red hair was so beautiful that she could not resist touching it again.

She stroked his hair lightly and let her fingers feel the fineness of it. The hair parted where her fingers passed through, and she noticed an odd lump on his scalp; then another lump. Pushing aside his hair carefully, she found four small red mounds on the top of Forrest's head, and she knew at once that she had to touch one. She pressed gently so as not to wake him, but a tiny shock coursed through her finger.

Forrest yelled like he had been stabbed. He smacked the wall over her shoulder with his open hand, leapt out of bed, and fell into a crouch, holding up his arms like a fighter warding off attack. His eyes were wild, his face frantic.

The violence shocked her, and she shrank away from him; but in a moment he straightened up, aware that he was alone with her. As the fear passed, she became angry that he had frightened her so.

"Don't ever do that," he said at last. He ran a wary hand over his hair and sat down on the bed beside her. The alarm had gone out of his face, but she was still too shocked to move, though she wanted to get away from him. A look of concern in his eyes held her and softened her slightly, and she was able to begin to come back to herself.

"What did I do?" she asked stiffly. The tone of her voice made it clear that she had not forgiven being unnerved by his incredible reaction.

"I'm very sensitive there," he said.

"But why?"

His brow furrowed with doubt, and he closed his eyes as if he were going over a great many possibilities. He opened his eyes again, but now they were drained, their purple depths oddly opaque. "Well," he said, "can I tell you later?"

"I think you should tell me now," Mary Alice said firmly.

Forrest closed his eyes again for a moment, then opened them and said, *"Iaii."* He slumped onto the bed and lay beside her as though the ordeal had overpowered him, and he fell into a deep sleep.

Forrest saw that he had to be more honest with Mary Alice, and he was. He worked to earn her trust, and a few months later they were married. Also at about that time, Schuyler & Blitz got a new name: Schuyler, Blitz & Pierce. Al Pierce, their boss, had become president of the agency after a series of dazzling campaigns from his department brought half a dozen major new accounts into the house. Marvin had been fired when he tried to claim credit for one of Forrest's ideas and was caught at it, and Mary Alice ran the meetings with Forrest's help. Together they had written a casino campaign that made 1001 Nights the hottest place on the Boardwalk. She had read Forrest a few tales from the *Arabian Nights,* and he said, "Just tell them they'll have that—the magic of the stories. That's what gamblers want."

Now, on television, Sinbad flew through the air on the back of a giant roc, the genie poured smokily out of the bottle, poor Ali Baba unlocked the treasure cave with "Open sesame," and the City of Brass glittered awesomely in the distance across a vast desert—all for the benefit of the 1001 Nights Casino. The three-hundred-pound client had disappeared, because business was so good that the real owners came forward to take care of things.

In addition, Mary Alice's Sunrise Cola commercials were such a hit that "old Roger" had doubled his billings. Between Forrest's salary and hers after the raise, they could afford a new apartment—two bedrooms, which cost a lot of money. They would move in a month, and there was a lot to do.

Shopping, for instance. Forrest usually stayed in the office when Mary Alice went off to Bloomingdale's or Lord & Taylor, because it was not necessary for him to go with her. He had been truthful about his *iaii,* as his antennae were called. They showed up only as small mounds on his scalp, easily hidden by a healthy head of hair, but they were both powerful in use and painful when touched. He let her look at them closely;

they were the only outward sign of his ear
to the minds of others, and they worked as
receptors and transmitters of thought.

Forrest knew that Mary Alice mistrusted
this power at first, but with nothing in her
mind that she did not wish to share with him,
she took his telepathic gift willingly and
made good use of it. She might sit on a new
bed in Bloomingdale's, letting Forrest see it
through her eyes and feels its bounce as her
bottom felt it; or, with an extra effort, he
could help her match fabrics from two different stores.

He had showed her he could read her
thoughts whenever he wanted to, and could
even put ideas into her head; but once she
understood this, he was careful to use his
power sparingly. He worked on advertising
ideas with her all the time, coming into her
thoughts so neatly that she took the ideas
as her own, until he gave her the signal that
he was inside her: a curling caress of her
lower spine.

Forrest gave Mary Alice lovely feelings, but,
of course, no real contact. He could not
afford to bring her fully into his mind just
yet—or maybe never. It would depend on
how far she could go in understanding him
without becoming upset. He wanted her to
come inside him, to see and feel who he
was, but he had to be very careful.

As for what he could do, he enjoyed flowing into her as a way of letting her know how much he liked her. Of course, if he had put it into words that way, she would have become hurt and angry. Mary Alice wanted to be *loved,* not *liked.* If he were too open and frank, she would leave him, and he could not let this happen. His time on this hot and teeming planet was much too precious.

Forrest had selected Mary Alice while the craft still hovered over Manhattan, and he had made sure they would meet when he caught and strengthened a playful impulse to leave her office and walk up Fifth Avenue. Later he had reassured her and held her steady so that she did not run away from the crash, and the pleasant sensation she had felt when she first saw him was simply one he had kindled when he found it in her mind. Heavier work, such as making the ship vanish or whisking himself and Mary Alice from the park to the office in a second—these things took help from the others, with whom he was in constant touch. They had all found mates and jobs and had begun the task for which they had come to this world. When any of the four had need, they could all stream their minds together and interlock their powers. Each had chosen a mate while still on board the craft, and each had arranged a casual meeting with the woman he intended to marry. Forrest had soon learned that crashing through a skylight was not quite casual, and he had passed this on to the others, but by that time they were all paired off.

Although Forrest had a lot to learn, Mary Alice was a willing mentor. At odd moments he curled a tiny tendril of his mind around the lowest bone in her spine; in effect, he tickled her tailbone, which he knew gave a warm feeling to most Earth mammals. She enjoyed it so much that at times she asked him for it when he would rather have let his powers rest. But he did it, too, because he really liked her.

A couple of weeks after they had begun living together, they were talking about the Martian language, and Mary Alice asked Forrest the word for *marriage.* It was a long compound word made up of several other words, and it meant, he said, "Drink at the same spring, breathe the same air, live under the same sky" and "Sleep as one and dream the same dream."

"That's nice," Mary Alice said. "And what's the word for *sex?*"

Forrest looked pleased, and he smiled. "You don't have the vowels to say it, but it's close to the other word. Literally, 'drink cool water together and be refreshed.' "

"That's not quite the way I see it, but go ahead and say it in Martian."

Forrest cleared his throat and with slightly

parted lips began to make a sound that seemed to be floating somewhere above his head. The sound was more of a wandering melodic tone than a sequence of distinct syllables, and it flowed around her for a moment like a playful breeze, then enveloped her and touched her all over. The tone changed shape in a way that made her think of a hidden stream whose headlong rush through a narrow passage is heard faintly behind the thick wall of a castle. In the space of a second or two the tone of the word moved between raw hunger and placid certainty, from posed question to pensive aftermath.

Mary Alice was silent for a moment when Forrest finished, and then she stood up from the sofa and walked barefoot across the room to where Forrest sat at the table by the window. She dropped firmly into his lap and said, "If that was a question, the answer is yes."

After they were married, Forrest had the impulse to tell Mary Alice the whole truth, as many newlywed husbands feel they must, even if they happen to be ordinary Earthlings; but he knew she could not live with the truth, and so he spoke to her of himself only as far as he dared. For instance, he had told her that his designation, 4-S-T, simply meant that he was the fourth member of a special team, and this was almost true; but he did not dare tell her that his age was 19,125 Martian years, which made him the youngest member of the group. Nor did he say that he and his companions could share each other's mindstream steadily so that each was aware of everything that happened to all the others.

As a matter of language, there was no Martian word for *other*. A long history of shared awareness had made the concept meaningless, although each of the four could screen out unwanted sensory impressions or unwelcome images from another's point of view. At the same time each could override the other's barriers in a flash if need be.

This mindstream power, which had been natural to all Martians for a million years, added to group awareness and built up knowledge even as it lessened risk. Nothing personal or unique could ever be lost. If one of the four on Earth died suddenly in an accident, or even in one of his rare moments of sleep, the total content of his memory and the meaning of his life would be sent in an instant burst of radiation to the survivors—anything, that is, which had not already been shared—and passed along at last to the ancient central mindstream back on Mars, where it would be kept fresh forever. A Martian might have the limitation of a particular body at birth, but his personality and awareness of himself was soon fully merged with the inner life of the rest of his kind, most of whom had "died" in the distant past. Since there were no true individuals in this shared sense of life, the problem of survival of the self could never arise, and no separation from group feeling was ever possible, nor was it desired. For a native the awareness of the group always began before awareness of oneself, and this made for an existence of unbroken euphoria. No one was ever bored. Life had not always followed this pattern on the planet, but such was the form of its adaptation a million years earlier, after the planet's second nuclear war.

Not much was known of their world's history before the Last War, as it was now called, but everything felt, seen, or understood by anyone since the onset of that watershed event had been set down and was held in eternal memory. The whole experience of the race now lived in a vast underground mindstream far below the dead surface of the planet, an entity with self-renewing life systems designed for its everlasting safety. The system drew power from the planet's electromagnetic field, and as long as Mars kept to its orbit, the mindstream would live.

Now and then, an individual Martian

might venture out to the deserted sands to see the lavender sky and once more breathe the thin, cold air, just to bring back a new sensation of things as they existed at that moment; but otherwise, little heed was paid to the outer life of the planet, which had been almost wiped out in that last conflict. In the aftermath the last sandbear had died over four hundred thousand years ago, and the ribbonbird not long after. But a charmed memory of these creatures, and others, would stay forever in the mindstream.

Ordinarily individual Martians, born telepathic, merged into the mindstream long before their bodies wore out from age or accident; anyone who wanted could simply lay aside his body like an old suit of clothes and live from then onward untroubled by the body's bounds. But how could someone like Mary Alice ever be expected to fathom and absorb this? Forrest knew it was not to be, and so he left out anything that would disturb her.

Recently, in a burst of curiosity, the mindstream had taken a look at all living Martians and found that the body-life of the species was dying from disuse. In fact, it was not needed, or the likely need was so remote as to be no worry at all. However, after a century of off-and-on notice within the mindstream, an understanding was reached that the species should guard against even the remotest chance of trouble that might take living bodies to deal with. They would try once more to create a new mindstream on another planet, one that would share the history and experience of the original on Mars.

Interbreeding with a local race already adapted to the other planet's environment seemed the surest way of bringing this about; and by great good luck the next planet in the solar system had such a race, though it was divided into many tribes and colors. The Mars mindstream had long since picked up a faint scattering of thought waves from the third planet circling the sun. A tangle of voices, images, and sounds gave hints of Ge, Erd, and other names, as Earth was called once its people began to grope toward a notion of whatever was beyond the familiar home range in which they lived.

However, this present effort was not the first time that the mindstream on Mars had decided to visit Earth. In fact, there had been many such times. The first was a brief close-up study of the planet half a million Earth years ago, and the outcome was most unpromising. The second visit took place only thirty-five thousand Earth years ago, when a survey team numbering a dozen was sent. At that time Forrest was too young to be touched by it, but he had checked all the memory traces from this expedition, sparse as the record was. The team had finished its survey and taken off on the flight home when the mother ship suffered a mishap that stranded the travelers on the eastern end of a large inland sea. The lost party had counseled against a rescue effort, and they remained on Earth to become the first colonists.

A report had come back in due course, brief because of the distance of transmission, and possible at all only because the twelve Martians had focused their powers on a single message. It had said, in part:

The local peoples treat us as gods. They give us their daughters and make sacrifices to us, abandoning time-honored beliefs and traditions. They bring us jewels and the finest produce of their lands, and masses of metal that they deem precious. Our natural powers amaze and awe them, and they seem likely to continue to deify us even after we are dead. No other task force is needed. If a mindstream can be created on this planet, we will do it. To hasten the interbreeding process, we each plan to live in a different land and take many wives to bear many children. We will see that our children intermarry in order to concentrate our strain, to improve the character of the population, and to breed a species possessing our unique powers. In addition, the intermarrying of our descendants will make peace between neighboring lands, and the cultures of this planet will thereby develop more quickly. If we are able to mate our children and grandchildren, those of our posterity who find themselves with our powers will take care to nurture their gifts in the same way.

Also, to lead these native tribes out of their cultural and intellectual poverty, we have told them that the power on the fourth planet from which we came is the sole good—by this we mean the mindstream, of course. We have taught the quick-minded among them the difference between planets and stars, and we have suggested certain configurations of stars as a way to mark the passing of time, the path of the Earth around the sun, and the procession of the seasons. These signs in the sky, we have given the names of familiar animals or commonly known objects so that they will always be remembered. As it happens, the planet has one star that marks true north throughout the year, and we have pictured a great bear as pointing toward that star.

In former times, these peoples have been aware only of events on Earth, but we have turned their gaze toward the sky, which now has a powerful attraction for them, because they know that we come from the heavens. This fascination will deeply influence their ability to sustain abstract reasoning and thus make them less Earthbound, particularly the new species we have engendered. Possessing superior brain capacity and bodily agility, they will no doubt replace the present population.

Forrest retrieved other information about the earlier expeditions, but there was little hopeful about what he learned. The powers of the stranded Martians had regressed when they went separate ways. Each sired hundreds of children, as planned, but separated by great distances, the twelve were forced to use their own telepathy sparingly, and so they devised a system of communication based on the twelve sky signs they had created. Each chose a sign to represent himself, and carved jewels were dispatched whenever needed, each with a telepathic message locked in its stony center.

The plan would never work, of course. Each tribe was too loyal to its own locality and its own kin, and the effort to bind them together by intermarriage failed after a few generations. Even though the first twelve outlived their earthly subjects by several lifetimes and so grew in authority and dominion, they could not control the course of Earth history. They became known as the Old Ones, the Elders, and when at last they died, their ages were exaggerated in myth and legend. Despite their brilliant genetic success with the new species of man, they failed to breed candidates for a mindstream.

But their offspring were clever, and with excessive cleverness came deceit. The crude, narrow, and uncaring moral outlook of the new generation did not bode well for the future of the species, especially since aggression had somehow been heightened. In a last noble act one of the Elders set down reasonable rules of conduct for decent behavior within the tribes, and his first rule was the abolition of carved images of life. The jeweled statuettes that the twelve had used had also provoked cults, and the mindstream in the sky was forgotten in the worship of a diamond ram, an emerald bull, or a sardonyx lion. Somehow Earthlings were captivated by appearances; they turned away from their own unseen forces in favor of the smooth and glittering surfaces that cunning craft made possible. Their fancy was taken with toys of the hand and eye, not with the mind's inward powers. Moreover, the special faculties of the "gods" were lost in the gradual dilution of key genes over generations. Now and then one tribal member would show unexpected powers of intuition, would divine men's motives and anticipate their actions; and such a man often became a leader, a warrior quick to surprise his enemies, or a courtier plotting to supplant his king. But in general the mindstream characteristics were overwhelmed, and the telepathic power could not be passed on consistently from one generation to another. This was the problem to which Forrest's expedition was to address itself.

Although the nurturing tried thirty-five thousand years earlier had missed its main purpose, hardly a day passed for Forrest in which he did not see some reminder of that failed expedition, and of the other later contacts. The hints were clear either in the physical makeup of someone he noticed or in some whisper of mind that alerted him by its familiarity. But these things were scattered, and a new mindstream could never be created from such wisps. The only hope for a happy outcome lay in four pregnancies that had not yet occurred. Before leaving Mars, Forrest and his companions had devised a two-step technique for directing a pregnancy to the end they desired—something the twelve had never tried. First, the ovum had to be telepathically probed when it was ready for impregnation in order to be absolutely sure that it had the genetic traits which would mix well with Martian sperm and allow telepathy to be dominant and not recessive. This was the easy part, because the ovum was fairly large, and there was only one at a time to examine. If it did not have the right aspects, there would be no impregnation. They would wait for the next ovum to descend.

The second step was more difficult—locating the strongest spermatozoon; that is, the one having the clearest telepathic signal. With millions of sperm to scan, Forrest and his companions had to work very fast.

Ideally this process required the husband to lie with his head on his wife's abdomen for several hours after making love. Since no normal husband could explain what he was doing in such a position at such a time and for so long, the wives became restless. Somehow this was not the course they expected a husband's affection to take. If necessary, they could be lulled to sleep for a while, but this took a lot of energy and was not always practical.

In the weeks during which Forrest was working to make Mary Alice pregnant, he had a chance to reflect on the differences between the humans of Earth and the *dawn firelings,* as they called themselves, of the home planet. Humans named themselves after the soil on which they stood, the earth that was their source of food and their final resting place; the Martian name came out of the awesome whirlwinds of fire that made up the Last War, when the race found a new beginning underneath the seared and broken surface of their world. They did not need the pale lemon disk of sun, lovely and cool as it was, to dispel the darkness of night. They had come to a miraculous inner dawn in the evolutionary leap of the all-feeling, all-seeing, all-accepting mindstream.

The safe possession and ongoing awareness of the entire mind-content of an ancient species had by now created an inner world so engrossing that the species had nearly forgotten that life was originally grounded in the physical. Death not feared or imagined might in this instance prove to be death triumphant. Certainly the mindstream would be safer with a twin of itself elsewhere in the universe.

When Forrest was reminded a few decades earlier that he still had a workable body that could be sent to the planet Earth to lay the basis for a new mindstream, he grew a shade uneasy, with a feeling unfamiliar to his kind—personal fear. He would be forty million miles away from the endless delight and total safety of the mindstream, and what if something happened to all four of the voyagers at the same time? What if the mindstream back on the home planet was too far away for a clear signal to draw their spirits back? But he understood the need to go, and his fleeting wish to be spared this task actually turned into a determination to see it through. The regeneration machines had made his body better than new, with a fascinating adaptation for sex with Earthwomen, and another for eating and digesting the astonishing variety and quantity of foodstuff that Earth offered. This was one of the big differences: the mindstream now lived on pure energy, whereas Earthlings had a clumsy and complicated way of sustaining the life force within.

But the chief difference between the two races lay in the abysmal loneliness of anyone born on Earth: Forrest saw humans as a race of cripples, condemned to a brief life of harrowing solitude of spirit, followed by the oblivion of certain death. In his experience at home no one was alien, no one was "other," no one was fallen away; on Earth all were alien, each cut off from the tree of life and destined to dwell forever inside his solitary self. It was easy to see why Earthlings tried to hide their condition from themselves, and why any reminder of their bleak inheritance left them angry and hurt, so that they developed devious responses to these feelings. The worst response was that they dulled themselves to their feelings in order to live in a pretended peace with their condition. Quite often Forrest felt the pain of those around him and so tended to withdraw, even as they did. However, he could never really believe himself alone, even when he parted from the mindstream on Mars, or when he was out of touch for an hour or two with the other three here on Earth who faced the same task as himself. All he had to do was open his channels, and he became part of the unseen life going on around him.

In the office and in his marriage to Mary Alice, Forrest had become an unwilling eavesdropper on the minds around him. It had been useful at first as a quick way of getting to know the people of this strange world in which he had to make a place, but the novelty soon palled, and much of what he heard troubled him. It was a shock to see firsthand the extent to which Earthlings deceived each other, at least in Manhattan, but even more disturbing was the fact that they so often deceived themselves. At last he understood that given the sour hopes of a life of enforced alienation, it was no wonder they spent their energies in a state of fruitless wishing or secret anger. Forrest saw too many smiling faces that masked interiors sick with rage; at other times the dull and ordinary spirit shown in a person's conversation was even outdone by the stony drabness of what was going on inside.

What was most absorbing to him was also the most disturbing: the coiled convolutions, the perverse and conflicting tides of feeling, the harsh push-pull of hidden purposes mostly unknown to the person himself. Humans were lonely and confused. Most of them could do no more than unravel the threads at the very entrance of the labyrinth of self before their attention glided involuntarily to another object. Fear made them ignore their own confusion or deny it; they could sprawl in the sun and not reach out for any more meaning than might be found in the nerve cells that lie on the surface of the skin. Their reasoning minds were true labyrinths that twisted on and on, riddled with dark corridors, deceitful byways, and dead ends, leading—but not leading—toward the killing beast hidden in the center, the half-man, half-animal that breathed hot anger, the monster they dared not find and face, who waited at their heart's core for his own death or the next victim. With every member of a species condemned to a known and personal death, no wonder they felt overpowering resentment, an impulse to strike back at life because their hold on it was so frail and fleeting. The people of Earth had minds within minds, an electric welter of tangled desires. All too often they lived like lonely, wandering monsters, vexed prisoners of their own desires. They rose up with their little flare of hope, glimpsed one brief flicker of the miracle of life, then fell back into the unforgiving dark. Would they ever find a way out of their confusion? Burdened with the double brain, would they ever recover from the trick life had played on them? The trick that made them the eternal Other, life unconnected, life outside itself? In their hearts, did they even *want* to survive?

To direct this race toward the blessings of the mindstream would be the greatest kindness he could ever do. And Forrest had chosen Mary Alice because she carried the least hidden resentment of anyone he had probed and was thus the least labyrinthine human he knew.

Forrest had taken to leaving the office early, usually before Mary Alice was ready to go, on the excuse that he would shop for supper. In reality he left early because it was so tiring to be pelted by the fears and angers given off by everyone around him. To avoid the rawness of it, he had to keep up his guard, and that was equally wearing.

One fine fall day he left his office a few minutes before five. He had held his powers in check all afternoon, and now he let his "bumps"—as Mary Alice still called them— idle casually, picking up mind patterns of anyone within wavelength. It was a relief to open himself up, and the effect at such moments was not nearly so bewildering as when he was trying to focus on a task in the office. He caught a babble of five o'clock activity in the ladies' room down the hall: a girl barely holding back hysteria would call in sick tomorrow because she had scheduled an abortion for ten A.M.; another young woman had fallen in love with a weight lifter and wondered what to do to make wheat germ tastier; somebody's poodle was constipated; and somebody else had pulled down her panty hose and was scratching with a relief that bordered on ecstasy. Stifled fear, an anxious hope, a petty annoyance, relief from a mild discomfort. Nothing out of the ordinary. Forrest and his companions had suffered at first from too much intimacy with Earthlings. How do you behave when what is said seems trivial compared with what you know has been left unsaid? He had to keep a distance from the seething cauldron of contradictions that he could find in most humans. One of the reasons he could live with Mary Alice was that she was not like that just yet, and maybe never would be. She actually approached self-acceptance, as difficult as that was for Earthlings.

As Forrest stood waiting for the elevator, he could make out the morbid fantasy of an account executive somewhere in the offices behind him. The man had two children, a wife in psychoanalysis, and a mortgage in Mamaroneck; and that afternoon some impulse had moved him to put his hand on his secretary's shoulder. She had treated the gesture casually, had shrugged him off but not moved away. Now the man was imagining what would have happened if he had followed his impulse and touched her breast.

Forrest turned his mind-probe away. He had caught a murmur from the agency president, Al, who was at that moment dropping swiftly to the ground floor in his private elevator:

stupid jerk drinking too much not pulling his weight really lost it in the last year why do I have to do everything myself?

The strong, familiar pattern faded as Al left the building, but the last wisp of thought carried the key to his character: it was the cry of one who kept on finding, over and over, that he was alone at the center of his world and had to hide this fact from himself.

Forrest felt relief when the elevator

came. A few minutes of looking into people, judging their souls—which was a sure post-script to insight—and then withdrawing to go about his own life was often as painful as not looking at all. He had had enough human static for one day.

A few weeks earlier, when Forrest had compared notes with the others about the puzzles of pregnancy, debating how they might control the second step of the pro-cess to get the outcome they wanted, he had held out for the view that they could not actually *control* pregnancy—they could only influence it. With so little time to set and guide the course of a single sperm swimming out of a throng of millions, how could they expect to do more than have a partial effect? But in that short period of time they had to use their utmost power. As he had said, "We'll just have to get in there and *push.*"

As it happened, that particular fall day had begun well: Forrest and Mary Alice had gone back to bed after an early-morn-ing jog. She was thinking about making a real breakfast for a change, but Forrest had said, "Forget breakfast. Why don't we . . . ?" She did not have to read his mind to finish his thought. Afterward, when he rested his head casually on her abdomen, he almost jumped with shock; a sound elec-trified him, one signal far stronger than the rest, the thin but unmistakable voice of a spermatozoon already somewhere near the head of the pack. At once Forrest used his powers of telekinesis to go inside and push the perky sperm along until it was a quarter of an inch in front of the surging crowd. He tried to keep Mary Alice in bed as long as possible so that the sperm would not be suddenly stalled by gravity as he headed upstream. But this was not possible.

Mary Alice tousled his red hair and said, "What are you doing? You're so strange!" She looked a little sleepy and was smiling at him.

"Getting closer to you." He did not want to explain what he was doing but was determined to keep his ear to her abdomen as long as possible.

"We were pretty close there a minute ago," she said, "but now I'm thinking about the office."

However, he quickly persuaded her to do a yoga exercise, standing on her head in the middle of the room, and then, with a superhuman summoning of his new human powers, he made love to her again. And with all of this they were still on time at the office.

Early that evening, Mary Alice came down the hall in their new apartment building while Forrest was putting the soufflé in the oven. Two nights a week, Tuesday and Thursday, he cooked dinner—a light supper, really, with a cold half bottle of white wine and a salad. His mind picked up her presence in the hallway before she came into the apartment; she was so pleased with herself and her life that the signal coming from her was like a fresh perfume. In that regard she was very much like himself and his companions. But today there was a difference; something else had been added.

Forrest was busy checking the heat in the oven and giving the soufflé mixture a final stir with his mind, and he paid little attention to Mary Alice until she was in the kitchen right beside him. He shut the oven door gently and turned to her. Then the difference hit him and almost paralyzed him with pleasure.

"You're pregnant!" he cried.

"What?" Mary Alice was startled, and he could tell she did not believe him. "How do you know?" she asked.

Forrest dropped to his knees and put his arms around her and pressed his ear to her belly. He could hear the faint life-murmur of the impregnated ovum clinging snugly to the wall of her uterus. Already the egg had a distinct sound, a clear sweet telepathic note like a high C. It was the same innocent tone one would hear in a Martian pregnancy, and he recognized it at once, having heard it summoned up many times in the mind-stream. Still on his knees, he flashed the other three and brought them in so they could hear what he heard. They hummed their pleasure and approval, and Forrest asked for a meeting later in the week when the four of them would get together in person and establish the kind of full mind-touch that worked best if they were within a few feet of each other.

Mary Alice had her hands on his head again and was not exactly pushing him away, but she said, "For goodness sakes, you're acting crazy again." Though she knew of his powers, she did not realize he could actually hear the life inside her.

Forrest stood up and hugged her, folding her in his arms as if he would never let her go. If he put his ear against the top of her head, he could hear all the way down to the little telepathic dot in her womb. He was very happy, the happiest since he had come here.

"Well?" she asked.

"I can tell." But he saw that her face was still filled with disbelief. "So go to the doctor tomorrow," he said.

Mary Alice smiled up at him and tweaked his ear. "That proves you're from Mars! No normal New Yorker expects to get a doctor's appointment just like that!"

· · ·

In a while he set their dinner on the table, and as they ate, they gazed out at the lights of the city, gleaming from the walls of buildings darkened by dusk. They talked about the office and what they would do if he were right and she were really pregnant. All the time, however, he could not help turning his mind to the tiny beacon broadcasting from deep within her, and he heard the change of tone when her cervix closed and the egg burrowed itself firmly into the inner wall of her uterus. If all was as it seemed, then he and his friends were on their way. By coming into his mind now and then during dinner, they listened with him, and all recognized the telepathic hum of a Martian mind in its very earliest stages, a sound that came from the germ-plasm itself before any other level of awareness had been reached.

As for Forrest, he listened intently to reassure himself that the good news was real, that the speck of life inside Mary Alice still pulsed with vigor. He wanted to monitor it constantly, but this was not possible. He had pushed the sperm toward its rendezvous but had missed sharing the moment of conception, though he knew what it was like: the delicate egg stood fast, waiting to be approached by a blind and blunt-headed fishlike creature that swam powerfully out of a vast darkness, lashing its demon-tail in a frantic race to reach the egg. The egg sent out a chemical signal that chose one sperm; other chemicals pierced the sperm's head and helped it penetrate the egg's outer membrane. Then suddenly the tail fell away, the head was wholly absorbed into the egg, and in seconds the sperm-creature dissolved as the egg took possession of its genetic material.

The Martian way—birth from the head, budding like a potato—was a little different, of course, but not so different that elements of it could not come into the mythology of Earth. Also, the Martian way took longer, occurred less frequently (though all three sexes could do it), and was not as wasteful. Incredible numbers of people populated this planet, each one sprung from the winner in a vast, muddled contest where only one sperm out of a hundred million could succeed. If the Martian strain ever got a good foothold here, where babies popped out of nowhere by the millions, there could be a thousand new additions to the mindstream. He and the others would have a lot to decide when they met in a few days.

In adjusting to the conditions of Earth life, the hardest thing for Forrest to get used to was his outsize body, and most especially the human body's digestive system. That long, winding tube was always at work, bulging and churning with what felt like a load of sludge. In its various parts the system sloshed and seethed as it pulverized, treated with chemicals, and soaked up great masses of Earth food. The mechanism of the stomach, with two conjoined wormy lengths of intestine appended, was not in principle different from the silicon-based digestive system of the Martians; but even sand digesting had been outgrown so long ago that it played no part in the metabolism of the mindstream, which took pure energy directly from the cosmos. Still, silicon was a lot less messy than the carbon-based plasms of Earth.

For Forrest and his companions it had been utterly impossible to start their Earthly digestive systems while they were still on Mars, and the same held true for the weeks in space. With all his knowledge of Earth, Forrest was still not quite prepared for what had happened on the first day, that time when he landed on the roof of the Guggenheim Museum and had dinner with Mary Alice six or seven hours later. For his human digestive system to work, Forrest's intestines had to be crowded with the common strains of bacteria that lived in happy symbiosis with their Earthling hosts. He took them in with his first meal on Earth, and he heard them growing in his abdomen as they multiplied furiously. In a little while it was as if he harbored a riot in his midriff. The bacteria went about their task, and since they were living creatures, they had feelings—conscious desires he could easily detect. EAT! EAT! EAT! they all seemed to be shouting at once. They lived and died by billions every day, and their constant racket was distracting. Now he could block out their noise and push it into the background, but in the first few days of being host to naturally greedy bacteria, their clamoring wore him down. Though the basic process in Martians was similar, there was a huge difference between the daily gorgings of humankind and the less than yearly feeding of a Martian, in which the waste matter from many months' supply of food was reduced to a single grain of transparent pink sand that dropped off like dandruff from one's scalp and was deposited harmlessly in a vast desert.

Life on Earth was extravagant and wasteful, shockingly prodigal, and it was also blind and intense. At home, life was neater, more complete, and much less demanding. Also, the powerful freedom of the mindstream fulfilled the promise of never being alone again and never dying. It was an outright, vigorous, and irrevocable connection, a lovely mingling with one's own kind.

One kind. One self. No separation. No death. Ever.

· · ·

Forrest shrank from feeling but could not easily avoid the sense of isolation enforced by his life on Earth. He could always activate his antennae for the other three, but he did so less and less because of the energy it took. He needed all the mind he could muster for life with Mary Alice, even though she was an easy person to be with, and for the problems in the office. Humans only knew life with a limit, life with a little fence around it, life canceled by the absurd invalidation of death. If Forrest and the other three could create people for a new mindstream, then a system following their own model, without death, could come into being on Earth. True, they had come to live almost as parasites amongst these Earthlings, but if they could fulfill their mission, Earth would begin to know eternal life.

Forrest and his friends could meet in many places, but they had already found the ideal spot. Four red-haired men, all looking almost exactly alike, would attract curious eyes if they met in a public place, such as a restaurant, and so they had taken to the serene darkness and welcome anonymity of a motion-picture theater. Comedies provided the best background for telepathic streaming, because the mental activities of the audience tended to flow in the same direction, focused and absorbed by the drama. The disorderly background static of a thousand competing voices was blended into a swirl of feelings that was often very pretty to see.

A week after Mary Alice became pregnant, Forrest slipped out of his office in the middle of the afternoon and hurried down the block to the Museum of Modern Art. He was a few minutes late, and damp from having been caught in a sudden shower. As he hastened down the stairs into the darkened movie theater where a film was already on the screen, he could "hear" the buzzing warmth of the mindstream that the other three had set in motion. A lightness of spirit came over him, a flowering of himself, a happy abandonment of all defenses, a mellowing-away of all fears. He was completely happy to be so close to the others and to see and feel so much all at once, and he slipped gratefully into the mode of mingled awareness.

Where he sat in the theater, or even whether he saw the others there, did not matter at all. The mindstream was an overpowering reality and tended to blot out everything else. The more reality, the better; together the four of them had a freedom and safety, a largeness of life, that none could know singly. The feeling was vast but at the same time intimate. Infinity in the mindstream was a personal sensation, not an abstraction, and the same held true for eternity. All was one—no pushing, no jostling, no regrets, no jealousy, no pride of place, no loss of any nature whatsoever.

Forrest stumbled across a man's feet and found a seat in the back of the crowded theater. Black-and-white images flickered and jerked back and forth on the screen, and people were laughing. If the images had flowed more smoothly, they could have been absorbed into the mindstream more easily, but they were kept at a distance. Near, but not too close. Even so, the images were intriguing. From a place safe within the mindstream, Forrest focused a particle of his attention on the figure of Charlie Chaplin, who at that moment on the screen had just bought a rose from a blind girl on a city street. The Little Tramp had fallen in love; he toyed with the rose and gazed at the girl in hopeless adoration. He stood near her, timid and worshipful. The blind flower girl fumbled to fill a cup with water, took a sip, and dashed the rest in his face. She did not know what she had done, and he could not cry out. A roar of laughter rose up from the audience.

why funny

The question rippled in the mindstream, provocative but awkward. It was an Earth riddle, not a Martian concern. Forrest did not want to consider the question and so came out of the mindstream once more into his human person; the move was like thrusting his foot into a shoe that would never fit. Dully he was at Earth-weight again, far removed from the bodily effervescence of many-minded pleasure. Something within the mindstream troubled him and made him ill at ease, and so he had come out of it. Now he found himself, heavy and solid, next to an overweight woman whose damp umbrella leaned against his leg and who had eaten something very garlicky in the last hour. He could have peered into the soupy mush in her stomach, but he refrained. Life on Earth remained a riot of sensation, and Forrest longed for the airy, floating friendship of mindstream-immersion he had known for thousands of years back home. What the four of them could do together was not good enough, though he needed it badly. And he feared they were growing weaker in their isolation from the mindstream back home. They might do a little better if they went away to the mountains, or to a mine shaft in a desert, but it would not be the same. Also, they had no time to waste; they had to complete their mission and return to Mars.

The garlic breath of the fat woman next to Forrest was unbearable, and he stood up and edged past her, muttering, "Sorry."

There had to be another seat somewhere in the theater, and a hint flitted out of the mindstream: "Third row." Perhaps the four of them had to be even closer together now to make their mindstream strong. He looked back and saw the other three seated just behind him, their faces totally void of expression now that all their feelings had gone into the streaming process.

On the screen, Chaplin had just jumped into the river to save a despondent but very wealthy man. In gratitude the man took him home and entertained him lavishly; the Little Tramp made himself comfortable on an overstuffed couch, crossed his legs elegantly, and smoked an enormous cigar, as servants in formal dress scurried back and forth to wait on him. But then the rich man came back to his senses, realized there was a ridiculous tramp on his couch, and kicked him out into the gutter again. Laughter rose up in the theater like a rainstorm on the roof; the man next to Forrest threw his head back, closed his eyes, and made a rapid, clipped barking sound. Forrest probed the man's mind but found no thought and not a wisp of sensation aside from the physical reaction of the barklike laugh.

There was no intellectual content at all, and it had been the same every other time Forrest had tried to catch the deeper meaning of humor; there were no clear clues to whatever had spurred the physical reaction. Of course, if an Earthling laughed heartily, he then became off-balance and ready for another laugh. Forrest had sensed this many times—the kind of frame of mind that looked to a repeated pleasure. He had even seen this in babies—there first, in fact—when the baby's parent was playing peekaboo. First the baby saw the parent's face, with glowing pleasure; then the face, especially the eyes, was hidden behind upraised hands, and a passing cloud of half fear, half wonder, shadowed the baby's expression; then the face reappeared, and the baby laughed with a pleasure so quick that his whole spirit swelled with it.

Was there a structure to humor?

together *abandoned*! together!

Or was it,

love *fear*! love!?

Forrest could see a model of pleasure/ *pain*/pleasure, with a rhythm in the playing out of the process. The pain was wiped out by renewed pleasure, but the second stage of pleasure had to be a surprise. In addition, this human reaction to anything comic had to be in large part unconscious, mainly grounded in the impulses of the unknown self that tended to dominate the emotional life of most Earthlings. But since the mindstream had no unconscious feelings hidden from itself, humor fell flat for them.

He reentered the mindstream to offer this point, letting the idea slip into the swirl of thought-play, the ever-living energy and rhythm that made up mindstreaming; but his notion came in too late to give new spin to the humor-eddy. The motion picture had flowed onward, and the mindstream hovered casually within its own sweet orbit, barely taking note of the image of Chaplin on the screen. The spiraling interplay of sense impressions, memory, and abstract concepts had now begun to circle around the notion of human love . . . huma lov . . . mlv . . .

love = mindstream   no no   we-all enter we-all   utter   pair-bonding motherchild   not like home   too much failurepain   re*ligion* = failure of love   hide unknown fear   deathalone   art = love   art = alone   can't enter utter like home

Forrest picked out some of his own thoughts swirling in the mindstream, but then wondered at himself for letting the word *own* come into his mind. It was there hiding in the language, ready to come out. This human language was tricky, words hid other words so that meaning spoke in many voices at once, from the same person, in the same speech.

He and his companions had no word for

own, either as verb or adjective. In fact, they had no grammar. Was this need for syntax in human speech beginning to change him, this talk-process that passed all impulses through the eye of a grammatical needle? Matching up language symbols— airy sounds—with solid realities in the human's outer world was an intricate game; but that was child's play compared to the inner struggle when people sought to find words to fit what they felt. They could rarely do it. Much language was a modulated scream, though few saw it that way or could bear to feel it that way because known anger made them fear to be alone again.

Language was a key force in shaping human personalities; the structure of language gave structure to the individual's developing mind. But the telepathic nearness of the Martian mind made grammar an intrusive nuisance. Why have an active verb when you can *show* the action and *feel* it? That was the beauty of the mindstream. Forrest had felt only a fragment of the group's handling of human love, but all parts of the fragment had come to life at almost the same instant, with no sense of time passing. Thought cloned thought; images and sense impressions fueled every phrase. For instance, the mindstream-image of "pairbonding" reached back to the first sexual feelings in infancy between mother and child and came down through puppy love, the sudden awakening and slow building of mate-love between a man and a woman (with the full range of sexual sensations of both), the sharing of birth, the growth of their child, and the final sad parting, when love still glowed but one of the lovers had died, leaving the other with memories that made the pain of abandonment cut all the deeper. These images took less than a second to be seen, felt, and understood in the mindstream.

Forrest cared enough for Mary Alice so that he sometimes wished he could focus himself within her mind to let her share his mindstream for a few minutes, to feel what he felt. In that instant she would know his inner life, but then all too soon his power to bring her into the mindstream would be drained, and he would be forced to break off. The loss would be dreadful for her. In one terrible wrench she would fall back into the desolation of her singular life on Earth, a state of which she was now mostly unaware. To live again on the angry planet Earth. Alone.

As for Forrest and the others, the makeshift mindstream they had been able to put together was just sweet enough to be a tease but not strong enough to sustain them at every turn in the world of these tumultuous humans, whose indwelling hidden selves made for a chaos of mixed motives in everything they felt. He needed to go home.

Mars was nearly sterile, with the purity of a desert and the starkness of desert life, and Forrest missed it. He missed the clean, cold air; the undemanding dazzle of a pale sun that looked like a baby moon in the lavender sky; and the abrupt, spectacular random flashes of laser beams set off by the sun's action upon elements in the upper atmosphere. Earth had its glories, but Mars was perfect. Most of Earth was a steaming jungle by comparison, and the people of this planet were like hidden traps waiting to be sprung. More than ever, he now saw that the buried pain of isolation, fearful of bringing itself into view, held sway in the hidden life of Earthlings and ruled them with the iron whim of an unseen tyrant.

The realization that Mary Alice was not quite like this had continued to grow upon him. His sense of her dignity was such that he became uneasy when the others in the mindstream wanted to know her sexually in the way he did, despite the fact that human sexual feeling was not a big thing to him. After all, it was mild, even bland, when compared to the never-ending pleasures of the mindstream. He held back because he knew Mary Alice would not want to be shared in this way, and her wishes were meaningful to him, insofar as he could honor them. In a sense he had begun to have a conscience about her, a psychic force that could not exist in the mindstream.

In his few months on Earth, Forrest had changed in another way: he had less of the erratic itch of Martian curiosity, which led to endless reflection. He could now merge his facts and guesses into quick action, and he could frame his actions on a time scale. In short, he could make a decision. The time for action had come, and this was itself a hard concept to grasp for a race with almost no sense of time. He turned boldly into the mindstream again and put the whole force of his being into a single message:

this is not what we are here to do

Shock rippled through the mindstream, and its swirl slackened. He felt the others focusing, those he could never think of as "others"; they now centered upon him and upon the startling break he had made in their mind-play. He was not sure how he had come to this point, but there was no need to search out the curious track leading to his decision. He began to "speak," and his manner of speaking did not allow for the usual interplay with his companions:

mindstream led astray   earth life
always alone unable to know

*mind of other or self   but can act
to purpose   we in mindstream lack
nothing   not   held   to   cause
never alone   no memory of alone
never to die   all pregnant now
we must leave*

All this Forrest said in a second, and it made a slow and shadowy moment in the mindstream as his friends held their silence. He pointed out that since the pregnancies had occurred as planned, the work could be finished. Soon Mars would pass out of the near range of its conjunction with Earth, and years would elapse before the two planets would again draw close to each other. And another dismal fact: their Earth bodies were not built for a long stay, and if they did not leave soon . . .

well   that's it

Forrest had made his point, and they were of one mind. As always. If they stayed another four years on Earth, their bodies might break down and become helpless. Unlike the earlier explorers, they could not adapt to a long stay. The resources to make this possible—the plasm, the bone—had been lacking, and because of that their plan had been to launch the new strain with four children only, strong specimens who would find each other and know what to do. This much could be arranged from home with a drone craft orbiting the Earth when the chil-

dren were five years old, if they had not
already found each other telepathically by
that time. The drone would be programmed
to bring them into maturity like a kindly
uncle, and the ship would not have to fight
Earth's gravity or return to Mars. The main
point was that the true children of Mars had
been conceived and that four fully telepathic embryos were in place.

 tell wives?

 no

They had agreed to leave in the seventh
month. That would give two months in the
embryonic stage and five at the fetal stage;
in this time the four would have a chance to
imprint their children with Martian knowledge and feeling, so that they could develop into true telepaths by the age of six.
Seven months was stretching the stay on
Earth, but Forrest and his friends could plant
the seed-model for Martian adulthood in
the children's growing brain cells so that
they could create their own mindstream. At
the end of the seventh month, Forrest and
the others would have just enough time to
make the Mars crossing safely. Meanwhile
their Earth life went on.

The day after making the decision to go
back to Mars, Forrest said to Mary Alice,
"There's something I think you'd like to

see." He was holding a copy of the *Times,* and he pointed to a photo from the current exhibit at the Museum of Natural History.

Mary Alice was eating a pickle-and-baloney sandwich an hour after dinner—owing to a sudden flare-up of appetite—and she had come in from the kitchen to peer over his shoulder. "The Ice Age?" she asked. "Whatever on earth for?"

He probed to see what she knew, but her mind was a blank on the Ice Age. However, now that he had raised the subject, he could not tell her his real reason; he had to shift his stance slightly. "I mean," he said, *"I'd* like to see it."

He probed again and saw that she had no resistance to the idea; the topic simply held little interest for her. At any rate, he wanted to lead her to some insight into that event, even if he could not say everything on his mind. She came around to the front of the chair and perched on his lap and said, "Okay, we'll go, but tell me about it first."

"Oh . . ." He hesitated. "We have so much in common with those people—you'll feel it when you see the show."

On Saturday afternoon they strolled through the permanent exhibits on the ground floor of the museum. Mary Alice was thrilled with the forest scenes—a scrubby timberline pine with bony branches tortured into a twisted shape by bitter winter winds, and a mountain lion poised watchfully beside it; a family of grizzly bears, with the male looming up fully eight feet tall as he gazed out over a lovely valley in which he and his brood might forage a hundred miles for foodstuff, while close at hand a beady-eyed chipmunk peered out of a rotted log; a colony of bedraggled beavers building a dam of gnawed branches to raise the water level of a slow-moving stream and hide the entrance to their lodges; two bull moose in mating season sparring awkwardly with huge, webbed antlers, while a pretty cow moose waited at a respectful distance.

Forrest had kept tuned to the undercurrent of Mary Alice's feelings as they walked along, and it buoyed him up to see that scenes like these made her grasp a big truth about life on Earth; she now felt in her bones the warm vein of kinship running throughout all of life, those webs of connection between living things that could be dimly sensed and deeply tugged. And she felt this despite what she saw in the exhibits of the age-old battle between species, the fight for survival that makes one creature see another as alien. The barriers marking off the animal kingdom from the human realm were not so clear-cut as she had supposed. This was one piece of what he hoped she would understand, and that much turned out to be easy because of her temperament; she had enough poise within herself to take everything to heart and not be the less for it. Her feelings were unguarded; she was touched by whatever she saw— including, on the far edge of what she could tolerate, the openmouthed shock and panicked eyes of a fat salmon that one of the bears had scooped out of a forest stream. When they left that exhibit, she hooked her arm through Forrest's to keep him close to her as they made their way along the darkened halls of the museum.

The dim lighting of the corridors worked simple visual magic to draw the visitor's eye into the scene-display, which by contrast was brightly lit from within, vaunting all the colors of nature. The glass wall that protected the exhibits somehow melted away as the scene itself took over one's imagination. There was real artistry in the putting together of these solid pictures of an instant in an animal's life. Each creature breathed its own air. If you were ready for it, your heart followed your eyes into the world of the animals; outside the museum walls, the crowded city of brick and piled-up concrete lay far behind, forgotten, as pure spirit flowed out toward life in the wild.

Forrest liked these displays, too, but was

more taken by the scenes of tribal life—a cluster of tepees on the Great Plains and a group of Indians getting ready for war; a hunting party of Australian aborigines trotting tirelessly across a parched stretch of outback under a cloudless sky and a merciless sun; African pygmies swarming over a fatally wounded elephant—these and others held his rapt attention. He wished he could see and record the whole human race, in all its astonishing variety, so much more diverse than his own people. He had spent two full evenings in the library and had flash-recorded over five hundred books, as well as twenty years of *National Geographic* magazine, for the benefit of the mindstream back home. Now he was dangerously close to overload, but he could not go back without scanning the museum, whose vivid scene-exhibits were magic windows offering an up-close look into far reaches of the planet. Most of all, he wanted to record and bring back the summing up of what the Earth now knew about the beginning of civilization and the end of its last Ice Age.

"It's late," Mary Alice said, looking at her watch. "Do you have the tickets?" They had just stopped in front of a wolf scene set in the Yukon. The wolf mother lay on a sheltered ledge watching two fluffy pups romping in cold sunshine, her mouth open in a way that made her seem to smile. A male wolf stood on the overhang above her, looking toward something happening down in the valley. Not far off on the painted horizon, another male wolf—painted in perspective so that he seemed to be a hundred yards away—lifted his leg to mark the pack's territory. Across the valley a herd of deer, tiny and remote, browsed beside a lake, while other wolves lay half hidden in the high grass, stalking the herd.

"Sure," Forrest said, taking the tickets out of his jacket pocket and showing them to her. Because of the crowds, the Ice Age exhibit could only be visited on a schedule, and their tickets were for four-thirty. Forrest's chief aim, and what he most wanted for Mary Alice, was to see the cave paintings of Lascaux. The cave site in France was now closed to the public because of air and pollution damage to the wall paintings, but this full-scale copy should be almost as good as the real thing.

At the entrance to the exhibit room, Forrest and Mary Alice joined a line of people slowly moving inside. There was a lot to see, most of it fragmentary, but everyone had to troop through the rest of the exhibit before getting to the cave. Forrest felt Mary Alice growing restless with the pace of things, and impatient toward the people

pressing around her. Besides, it was hard
for anyone except specialists and scholars
to care about a series of bone needles and
flint fur-scrapers. However, the bone spear
handles were quite beautiful. Several were
carved in the shape of the kind of animal the
spear thrower wanted to kill; and the handles were cleverly contrived to flip the spear
with greater force and accuracy than could
be done with the unaided hand. Also, there
was a skin-covered hut with hides stretched
over a framework of mammoth bones and
tusks, and this stirred Mary Alice's curiosity
because she could feel what it might have
been like to live in such a hut in snow and
cold.

They stopped to look at a reindeer bone
grooved with microscopic carvings of the
phases of the moon, and Forrest pointed to
the skill of the work and what it meant.
Whoever carved the bone had eyes so
sharp, he could see things that anyone now
would need a magnifying glass to make out;
and also, the carving on the bone traced
the waxing and waning of the moon. The
bone could have been used as a kind of
monthly calendar to mark for the people of
the Ice Age the passing of seasons, and the
coming of winter or spring. . . .

In an alcove near the cave, Mary Alice
and Forrest came upon a row of glass cases
holding a dozen figurines of the female
body. Some of them had huge, drooping

breasts, as well as hips and buttocks piled up with fat to a point of deformity. These little goddesses were a caricature of all females; they lacked individual faces, and their sexual anatomy was grossly overstated.

"I don't like them," Mary Alice said. She wrinkled her nose and held out a piece of literature she had just picked up. "This pamphlet says these things probably have nothing to do with fertility," she said, somewhat doubtfully.

"I'm sure you're right," Forrest said, reading her skepticism. "I imagine they were given to women to handle like an amulet—you can see most of them were meant to be passed hand to hand. The feet are wrong for standing up in a shrine. They could be held and prayed over whenever a woman wanted to become pregnant." He flashed an image to Mary Alice: a half-naked woman kneeling in a shadowy cave at nighttime, by the flickering light of a fire; a shaman, his face hidden within a bear mask that covered his head and shoulders; he hands the woman one of the figurines and she fondles it, her lips moving in a prayer, then lies down on a pile of furs with her mate, who has been waiting on the outer edge of the firelight.

"*That's* interesting," Mary Alice said, squeezing his arm.

. . .

At last their turn came to enter the cave, whose walls of dun earthen papier-mâché made a cramped, hollow space in the midst of one of the museum's great halls. Forrest had read up on Lascaux and saw that the exhibit room would have been hopelessly jammed with a crush of people if the long, narrow passage leading to the real cave had been copied there. Any Ice Age native who came into the cave at Lascaux for the first time would enter the vast body of Mother Earth and then grope down through a dark tunnel toward the mystery within; and the dread prompted by this entry would make him ready for the awesome beauty of the cave paintings. Simply walking through a door, as in the exhibit, would never do it. One needed to be aroused by the darkness and uncertainty of passage before coming out into a lighted chamber whose walls were alive with painted animal figures.

Forrest could tell that Mary Alice was missing the drama of the cave and the witchcraft of the paintings; and so was everybody else. Many of the animals were stunningly sketched, handsome in their spare stroke work and sharply picked-out detail. With their economy of means— chalk, ocher, charcoal—they might have been drawn as hastily as graffiti; but they were quick studies from life, with the simplicity and strength of great art. Even in the glare of the museum's overlighting, the figures came across with a lifelikeness that set the animals in front of your eyes; but by the shifting yellow glow of an oil lamp they would have looked ready to walk off the wall.

That deer was *that* deer and no other, not some vague abstract of all deer. That dancing shaman, with jutting rump and masked head thrust forward, had bent his body into an exaggerated posture like a Kabuki player; but he was a real man who had lived and died, a man whose ghostly eyes peered directly at his onlookers and demanded that their souls pick up the rhythm and verve of his movements, that they sway with him to know what he knew and feel what he felt.

Forrest was busy recording all of it for the mindstream, but at the same time he could hear the coolness in Mary Alice's mind. She was only mildly taken by it all, and that was far from what he had hoped. Why did so many things go wrong here on Earth? Why was it so hard for people to muster their strivings toward a chosen goal? Hardly any of them ended up doing what they meant to do; no, they found what they wanted at last, after a fashion, but most of the time they did not know what they truly meant to do—or, rather, knew only a part of it, so that the outcome was at odds with whatever they first imagined they had meant. Forrest knew what the painters of Lascaux had meant to

do, and of course they had failed; their
animals, sketched from life, were scattered
helter-skelter, as it seemed, drawn at different times and by different hands. The
figures ran along the walls in no detectable
order and floated overhead, real in feeling
but cut off from a real setting. However, he
knew the underlying reality and wanted
Mary Alice to know it, too, even though he
could not reach this end except by going
into her mind in a way he did not want to
do.

"I'm tired," she said. "Let's go home."

Outside, in the warm fall afternoon, they
walked toward Broadway to take the bus
downtown; but on Columbus Avenue, Forrest suggested that they stop at an outdoor
café for coffee. Mary Alice had brought
along a pamphlet from the exhibit, and she
started to read bits of it aloud while they
were waiting for their order. Her conscious
interest still touched only the surface, but he
was surprised to see her being drawn into
the subject by a curiosity that made her
want to fathom what she had seen.

The Cro-Magnons, or Homo sapiens,
*most likely originated in Southern Africa
a hundred thousand years ago; however,
they are best known for the suddenness
with which they appeared in Europe and*

*repopulated that continent in more re-
cent times. They replaced, though we do
not know how, the population then native
to that region, the Neanderthals. This
occurred during the fourth glaciation or
Reindeer Period, so called since reindeer
were so plentiful in that time. Cro-Magnon people invented language, art,
music, dance, a class system in society,
and probably trade. They are the imme-
diate ancestors of modern man. With
surprisingly large brain capacity (1550–
1750 cubic centimeters), and with most of
the enlargement coming in the cerebral
cortex at the front of the skull, they were
capable of high intelligence. In fact, their
brain development exceeds the capacity
of modern man, whose brain size aver-
ages 1350 cc. In a few millennia they
perfected many simple tools already in
use and little changed for millions of
years by* Homo habilis *and other early
ancestors of the human race.*

She looked up from the pamphlet and set
it aside as a waiter rattled coffee cups near
Forrest's ear. "So why," she asked, "do
they think we came from these people if
we've got smaller brains? They make it
sound like we've gone downhill."

"You might think that," Forrest said, not
knowing what to say. He couldn't really go

into what was on his mind, and why did he want to, anyhow? Her face was puzzled; she was so easy to read that it almost unnerved him. Mary Alice had quickly grown to be totally straight with him and with herself, able to let most of her feelings come to the surface; and the reason was the very fact that she had come to trust him so deeply, which he had encouraged her to do. He had won her over almost too well, and her openhearted reliance on him made him want to be worthy of her trust, made him want to tell her as much as he could so she might be better able to cope with the loss of him, her husband, when he returned to Mars. At this very moment she believed she had no worry, that he was forever in her life, in their life together. And all the time he had was just under seven months.

"I'm glad you wanted to see the Ice Age," she said, stirring a dot of cream into her coffee. "I wonder what the cave and the paintings meant to those people?"

Forrest looked into her lovely face and reached for her hand in a gesture he regretted as soon as he felt how much she liked it. "I'm thinking about it," he said. Before he left for good, he would have to try again to say more of what he knew and who he was.

However, a few weeks later something happened. At the meeting in the theater, the plan had been easily worked out, but now everything was changed. When this unforeseen event came to pass, Forrest hurriedly held a round-robin with the others, and all agreed upon the next step.

The time was late October, and Forrest suggested to Mary Alice that it would be nice to spend a weekend in the country. She thought it was a wonderful idea. Her pregnancy had not yet begun to show, except in a glow of good health and in her cheerful frame of mind. She smiled a lot and was very peaceful.

They left the city at noon on a Friday and went to stay at an inn on a pretty lake in northwestern Connecticut, where the trees had come into full fall coloring a week earlier. Whole forests of maples were red and yellow in the bright weather, at their dazzling best, as if their glory would never end. On the first night the sharp air warned of winter, and Forrest probed a weather satellite passing over northern Canada. A front was moving down swiftly, with a cloud pattern that looked like a huge bird whose wings would soon subdue the landscape. Forrest and Mary Alice slept under a down comforter, which they drew up snugly against a restless breeze that tossed the curtains at open windows.

Mary Alice woke at daybreak, and the transition in her brain from a serene alpha rhythm to a quicker beta pattern brought Forrest awake as well. He had not really slept, since sleep was rarely necessary for him, and he often spent quiet nights in the little mindstream with the others, if they were in range.

The day was too good to waste, and Forrest and Mary Alice dressed quickly and went downstairs. The dining room was quiet, orderly and empty, its air fresh because of a window left open all night. It was a small room; five tables stood ready, with crisp white tablecloths and napkins folded in peaks, waiting for breakfast guests. In the empty kitchen just off the dining room, the only sound was the whispered hum of a refrigerator. A gray tabby cat lay on a pillow next to the refrigerator, regarding them in silence with eyes that showed not the slightest trace of curiosity. Forrest saw she was picturing a prowl around the yard and hedges of the inn, and he unlatched the back door and held it open. She stood up, stretched her body, and padded out the door without glancing at him, her tail held high.

"I'm hungry," Mary Alice said. She didn't really have to say it; her appetite had grown visibly in recent weeks.

"Madame must have overslept," Forrest said. The woman who ran the inn had fought in the kitchen last night with her husband the chef. Forrest had brought in the mindstream for both the passionate fighting, most of it in French slang, and the even more passionate making up in bed after midnight. Now, on the third floor in their bedroom, the husband still lay snoring on his back, while Madame stood in the shower soaping her breasts. She thought of the night before but dismissed it with a smile and a little shrug. Through her eyes Forrest looked out the bathroom window; the peaceful surface of the lake, gray in morning light, suited the calmness of her mood, while the warm shower spray made her back tingle. She was friendly and poised for a busy Saturday; this was a morning she would make breakfast and let the poor man sleep.

Madame would not be downstairs for at least another half hour, and Mary Alice needed something now. Forrest probed the contents of the refrigerator and found oranges. He opened the door, took out the three best, and sliced and squeezed them. In a few minutes Mary Alice smiled at him over her glass.

"I don't have to ask you for things," she said. "It's wonderful."

She had awakened from a deep and restful sleep, ready for a huge country breakfast. The fresh juice would at least take the edge off her appetite until Madame came downstairs. In the past month Forrest had controlled the morning sickness so that she never felt it, and she was putting on a little weight. Her face was full and rosy, so much so that everyone in the office remarked on it. She looked prettier than he had ever seen her, and her hair took on a deeper glint of red in the morning sun as they sat on a fieldstone terrace facing the lake. Madame came down at last, her short-cropped hair still damp from the shower, and busied herself in the kitchen.

After breakfast, Forrest and Mary Alice set out to walk around the lake, now glistening in the risen sun. Stiff brown sedge grasses skirted the north end of the lake, and Forrest casually probed there for fish. However, the temperature of the water, always cool, had dropped just enough to put the fish into hiding. Fish did not "know" that winter was coming, but their bodies knew and acted to move them to deeper waters to stand off the onslaught of freezing weather. Mary Alice's body was now likewise working from its own knowledge. Forrest could track the busy hormones and the million little changes taking place as she grew with her welcome burden of life, changes still not in plain sight except as her limitless sense of well-being. She was happy all the time, giving herself over to the life slowly unfolding within her.

However, it was much too early for her

to have any special feeling of motherhood; that would come later, but for now Mary Alice was content to be a channel of the force of life rushing through her. She would become busy in a new way when the bodily parting from the child took place at birth. The bonding of emotions, one person to another, never would have been needed on this planet if mother and child were not torn apart each from the other at birth; but when they went through that wrenching change, that fish-out-of-water lurch to a new reality of life, feelings sprang up that soothed the pain of loss. New pleasure lessened new fear. This one-to-one linking took energy and time and added a stamp of character on both sides, but the demanding intricacy of caring about another person meant that all humans in later life had only a handful of others upon whom they could rely, no matter how wide the sweep of their sense of care. The bonding pattern with the mother—and with the father, too—would mold the drama of the child's later bonding with others and the way in which he cared for himself.

Mary Alice, like most mothers, would come soon enough into the clear light of her own loving need to mother the new life that life had placed in her care. Her pregnancy was a fact of nature, and its pleasures would be rounded off with a little pain; she would stay mostly passive in this time, while all the systems of her body worked in active harmony to create life. To become a mother lay in the realm of nature and took nine months for humans, but the condition of motherhood lasted a lifetime—even beyond the point where mother-wisdom said, "Let go."

Motherhood was nurture, plain and simple—and not so simple. At the moment of need, Mary Alice would feel the call of her own soul to watch over, to nourish and to protect their growing child; and as the demands of nurturing grew more complex, she would look into her own growing spirit to find what was needed. It was a very bad thing that Forrest would not himself be on hand for her and for his child; every time he looked at Mary Alice pregnant, he wished he could stay, and with every wish he felt a pang of grief, an emotion that had no place or parallel in the mindstream.

Forrest had loved to watch the day-by-day growth of the embryo, which was breathtaking even at this early stage. He could speak with his child and nurture his mind in the Martian way, at the same time himself floating in embryonic bliss within the womb. He and his son—he had decided to have a boy—made a little mindstream together, since it was never too early to bring a child into this way of life.

However, the day before yesterday something terrible had happened. Mary Alice had been lying with her face on his chest, as she often did just after making love. His senses rocked idly along, calm and casual, picking up nearby trifles that took little exertion. With no warning at all, the signal from the embryo abruptly wavered. Forrest caught the wisp of a new tone and dived into the child's mind. He saw at once that disaster had befallen; it was the worst possible turn of events: the embryonic brain cell with its unique *dawn fireling* personality already clear and active, had suddenly split in two. With this development, it was certain that his child would be born with the double brain of an Earth person rather than the single but many-layered lobe of his own kind.

Inside an hour, the lively telepathic signal had faded into a feeble blip, falling off into the hit-or-miss cycle of mere Earth genius. This was a shock to Forrest on a level deeper than the failure of a mission: his offspring, his very own child, might be capable of dazzling intuitions, might even be able to understand himself; he would have wide-ranging artistic gifts, as well as moments of clairvoyance. But now and forever, he was deprived of the sure powers of home. For his son there would be no telepathy, no telekinesis; and worst of all, he would never have the chance to lose and find himself in the fullness of the mindstream. Forrest had risked the dangers of absolute zero and the relentless vacuum of space, had come forty million miles to this alien planet, and now, for the first time, he tasted despair.

Less than an hour after that point, the other three had signaled to say that their embryos had also slipped over to human brain cycles. Forrest joined with them to probe the DNA helix to puzzle out what had happened, but the twisted chain of causative protein was too tiny, too complex, too exhausting to decipher. The wellsprings of the central mindstream back on Mars would be needed for such a job. But they could guess the terrible truth, even though they could not see it: that some brutal chromosome in human genetic makeup had overpowered the Martian factor. It was matter over mind, even though mind was merely matter that could think. And the minds of this planet lay trapped in their own chemistry, imbedded in a wet system that managed to reach pure radiation frequencies only at odd times. On Earth, Earth chemistry prevailed, and kept minds earthbound.

The experience of Forrest and his friends was now consistent with past efforts to create a genetic colony. The attempt to graft their planet's strain to the population of this globe was their noblest idea, but it would never work. Or at least, only partway and in unforeseeable paths. Forrest's son would grow up to be a person of great ability and renown, but he would still be human in every sense of the word. A single soul; lonely; victim to the usual death.

There was no point in staying on Earth any longer; they would not wait for the seventh month of pregnancy but would go back to Mars at once. The other three would have done it on the instant, two days earlier, but this was too sudden for Forrest, who wanted a little more time with Mary Alice. Time in which he would resolve the question of how to leave her and what to say. She was pregnant and he was leaving, and he had to soften the blow, for her sake, for the sake of the child. The human body was driving him now; it was odd, but when you took on this flesh, life in this strange form, you were in danger of becoming human yourself.

Also, he was leaving with more failure to his account than could have been imagined when he spoke to the mindstream that day in the theater. He had never told Mary Alice the most piercing detail of his plight—that he and his companions were the last four men on Mars. A handful of others had not finally disposed of their bodies, but they were too old for the trip, even with the best efforts of the regeneration process. And he was sad, finally, because the people of Earth would now be left to their own devices, with no more help or intervention from the wiser and older race of home.

"Look!" Mary Alice cried, shielding her eyes against the morning sun, her face upturned to the sky where a flock of geese flew in a V-formation overhead, their long necks firmly stretched and pointing south, their wings pumping smartly in the clear air. Forrest did not have to probe them to hear their friendly honking as they urged each other to keep close in line on their southward migration, but his curiosity drew him into the mind of the goose at the point of the *V*. The view was superb, the air buoyant beneath his wings, the power of flight exalting. Beneath him lay a wide and familiar landscape, with trees and fields and houses and, now and then, people and cars. The flight of geese had already passed over, but Forrest turned the goose's head so that he could see himself and Mary Alice far down below, tiny figures on the edge of the lake, almost lost in the sweep of the landscape. They were hardly worth noticing.

But when he saw Mary Alice shrunken to a stick figure in a vast perspective, the stab of concern rose anew in Forrest's mind. Why should he care what she felt when he was gone? The insurance had been arranged, and he had made an investment that would pay off handsomely within the year. True, she would have no help from him in raising the child who was half his, but she could easily take care of herself and the baby with the provisions already made, the same as the other three wives. Nevertheless, disquiet nagged him. It was not just a question of money, but of having been dishonest with someone who trusted him; and he was abandoning her at the very moment she was embarked upon the creation of new life. Her own baby; and his.

What he was about to do would be devastating, and Mary Alice would suffer more than he cared to think about. With his own kind, a feeling for each other was instantaneous and total, but sharing the feelings of Earth people had to be learned because they were so different, crude, and incomplete. Perhaps he had made a greater effort with Mary Alice than the others had with their wives, but there was no question—he had become bonded to her.

Of course, he might have gone into her mind and fiddled with her feelings to short-circuit the sense of loss once he was gone; he could condition a response so that she smiled and felt happy every time he came to mind. But in his brief stay on Earth he had come to like Mary Alice enough to want her to know who he was and then reach an opinion of him on her own. It could only be mixed, at best, but he wanted it that way. If possible. But it was still not within reach. Once he had stood in the Metropolitan Museum with her and gazed for a time at a lovely Madonna and Child. He had tried to help her feel both minds, baby and mother, from the inside and at the same time. He wanted to lead her to an analogy of the mindstream, but of course he could not do it. She would never know what he had risked to come here, and if he stayed, he would waste away and die within a few years. And what good would it do? Was hurting her part of what he had to do? He had come to feel that being hurt was in the very nature of being human. These people had to take the pain of their condition and make the best of it, simply in order to be themselves, separate and alone.

Forrest and Mary Alice chatted as they made their way along the lake's edge, and in a couple of hours they had hiked all the way around and back to the inn, where they were just in time for an early lunch. Afterwards, they went to their room again for a nap, and when they woke up, they made love twice before dinner, even though Forrest was having a hard time disguising his troubled mood. It was a sunny afternoon, but they stayed inside a room that had become a place where time had stopped. They would hardly have known the day was passing except that Mary Alice had turned on the radio to a classical music station, and stately sounds issued faintly from a far corner of the room. Now and then the music paused for a news broadcast, but they were oblivious.

Dinner was also early, and by candlelight, even though the sun had not quite gone down. Only one other couple was staying at the inn, and they had not yet come in to dinner. At this time of the year the inn's season was almost over, and soon Madame would pull her shutters closed and take no more guests until spring. Mary Alice leaned toward Forrest over the table and whispered, "Do you think they'll let us come back with the baby next year?"

Forrest raised his eyebrows and shrugged. "Maybe renting a cottage for a month would be a good idea," he said, changing the subject slightly. He cared for her and for his Earth child, but by the time spring came, he would be millions of miles away, safe once more in the euphoric life of the mindstream. He looked at her face, so pretty in the candlelight and so happy with everything that was going on in and around her, and it was almost too much to bear. He could not help picturing her anguish, of which he would be the cause. *Firelings* were not suited to the burden of individual life, and it would be a relief to give it up, this condition that left all humans helplessly entangled in time and fated to hurt each other. With minds unfit to read the inward life of another person, they shared feelings only in the clumsiest of ways and so were denied the fullness of life's reality—so strictly denied that from an early age most humans learned to avoid hurt to their own feelings by denying the bonds of kinship and relying instead upon abstract ideas about life. To be all human was to be half alien.

Desires became motives, and thwarted motives turned into fiery burdens of angry desire, buried but still smoldering. Unreached goals changed form and became defenses against the desire to reach these goals, and the power to reason became the power to excuse oneself for failure. And all because the realities of life and death in a solitary state had to be avoided at all costs.

Any true vision of life, whether human or his own, was prompt and involuntary—reality had to be seen for what it was before the overlaying of one's will or desire disguised it. But one's subtle displacement of reality by a will working in the service of hidden desires needed further and constant efforts to keep up appearances, inner and outer—even if those appearances were supported by history, tradition, ritual, and the approval of family and society. In contrast, the mindstream was totally honest and therefore managed to unite self, family, nation, race, and species into a single living organism. Neither government nor social contract had been needed for a million years, and manners could not even be imagined. Their society was perfect in fact and in feeling; finished, yet endlessly new.

Mary Alice was yawning from the effect of half a glass of wine with dinner, and from the fresh air. She was ready for bed again by the time dessert came to the table, and she smiled at him after a few bites of apricot tart and said, "Okay?" He held her chair as they left the table, and then they took a turn around the yard in the last fading glow of sunset.

Upstairs in their bedroom, Forrest sat in a cushiony armchair by the window with the mug of coffee Madame had handed him when they passed the kitchen door on the way to their room. From the chair he watched as Mary Alice undressed, put on her nightgown, and combed her hair. He had started to read a volume of short stories by de Maupassant, but he lay the book, open pages down, on the table. The man was too unsettling for this moment, too much attuned to the ironies of human life.

The sun had gone down at last, and an astonishing expanse of pale orange sky stretched over the woods on the other side of the lake. Soon the colors faded into a gathering darkness that went from blue to near black as he watched, sipping coffee from the still warm mug. There was no moon yet, but the stars came out sharp and bright, like jewels strewn carelessly here and there by a hand too rich to reckon the cost. His planet hung over the lake in the west, brightest object in the sky, and it had that passing tinge of red that never failed to stir his desire to go home.

"I think I'll step outside for a few minutes," Forrest said. He closed the book and set his mug on the maple end table beside it.

"Come to bed soon," Mary Alice murmured. She had slipped under the covers and was already drifting off. She had turned on her side so that her face was away from the light, and her neatly combed hair fanned out on the pillow. He switched off the lamp and cast the room in a soft darkness. She would be asleep before he got downstairs.

Outside, in front of the inn, Forrest stood on the terrace for a few minutes, listening to the sounds of the earth, then walked down to the edge of the lake. The only other guests, a middle-aged couple, were playing canasta in the living room, and light from the windows came all the way down to a slatted boat dock belonging to the property. A small rowboat lay in the water, tied loosely to the dock. Forrest scrambled into the boat, unlooped the deck rope, and pushed off into the lake. The boat floated lazily away from shore and coasted in slow silence on the still, glassy surface. He looked down into the black waters as the boat glided through the wavering reflections of stars. It was peaceful here, not a cloud in the sky anywhere; however, seventy miles to the south, Forrest knew that a thunderstorm bristling with lightning had almost reached New York. The storm had been whipped up as a cover for the spacecraft, at this moment being summoned from orbit to fetch him and the others and take them home. Everything was ready.

Except that Forrest was not ready.

He looked into the darkened upper windows of the inn and thought of Mary Alice. He focused into the bedroom and saw that her breath was regular and that her eyes moved rapidly beneath closed lids in the early stages of sleep.

She was having a brief happy dream of playing with a puppy on the lawn of her home back in Ohio, and the puppy was nuzzling her face with his warm wet nose as she stepped firmly onto the escalator rising to the top floor of Macy's department store on Thirty-fourth Street in New York, where she meant to buy a new dress and a jeweled brooch in the shape of a bird. Forrest stopped his probe and let the picture fade. Why was he going into her mind now? It was much too late to change anything or make amends for what he was about to do. He let his mind drift, and he floated by dim starlight on the glassy dark lake. Its surface, so smooth in the unearthly stillness, lay around him like a vast, stretched membrane in the perfect isolation of the night. He was a speck floating on a mirror reflecting the universe so that the universe could see itself.

But seventy miles to the south, the roiling storm cloud drew near New York. What could he do? The others were leaving their wives without explanation, but somehow he had to tell Mary Alice. He could not simply disappear and leave her sleeping in a happy dream, only to wake later and find him gone, with nothing left behind but a billfold in an empty rowboat drifting on the lake.

shall we?

They were calling him. The voice of the mindstream had broken his reverie. The others were ready to start, to meet in Central Park about a mile from where the craft had first landed on Earth. It had been waiting unseen in orbit for five months, undetectable by the radar systems of Earth where it circled in space, always just the other side of a dead satellite. Now it had been summoned to the coordinates of Sheep Meadow in Central Park, a spot already cleared of people by the rain and hail running just ahead of the thunderstorm that cloaked the spacecraft.

wait Forrest said   *a few minutes*

He was still not sure what he wanted to do, but he unshipped an oar and dipped its tip into the starry, glass-dark water. His paddle disrupted the dreamy glints of starlight and stirred the lake's calm surface. He could have flown bodily to shore with little effort, and from there into the upstairs bedroom, but he wanted to sit and feel the normal pull of gravity and let everything on Earth pour into his soul for one last time. The lake's illusion hung beneath him like another sky, this one also falling away deep into the well of infinity, and he dangled lazy in space, wishing he might be forever still in spirit. But he had much to do, and with a reluctant touch of his oar he paddled through stars.

As the boat moved, Forrest opened his mind to the strange forms of life on this alien planet. They had something to tell him that he wanted to take back home. A few feet below the keel of his boat, three small perch idled aimlessly, unaware of a murderous, hungry pike cruising nearby. He had seen this kind of Earth drama too often, and he deflected the pike to another part of the lake. As he came near the dock, he focused on a shallow place where the waters were sheltered, and he saw thousands of parameciums darting and twisting. They looked like silver slippers come to life, fragile in body but wild and cheerful in spirit. He homed in on one, more acrobatic than the rest, and tasted tiny bits of algae in its oral groove. The creature's whole nerve system was electrified by the desire to eat, and a non-pattern of tricky random movements tested his skill to stay locked on while it rotated, whirled, wove in and out, and foraged insatiably for food.

At last the boat touched dockside, and Forrest stepped out. The windows of the inn were all dark now, but he did not need their light. He walked up into the yard, where he could hear the tangled murmuring of worms that burrowed underfoot throughout the lawn. There must have been a hundred thousand earthworms within range. He paused for a moment, then knelt and put his ear to the ground, and the sound was like a slow, heavy breathing. He found a worm a few inches away and on impulse slipped into the creature's body. Though blind, it "saw" well enough with touch, smell, and taste as it went about an endless task, absorbing dirt with its mouth, boring a tunnel to nowhere. But he suddenly realized that this one was rushing somewhere, an inch an hour; the creature had picked up the scent of a ball of copulating earthworms a foot away and hurried to join his tunnel to theirs before the complex orgy of creation was over. Forrest dipped for a moment into the soft, twining tangle of worm bodies. In later times, when he could no longer join them, he would recall the glow of their slow, friendly pleasure.

He stood up at last, ready to probe a tree. When he had first explored plants, back in June, he found that he could feel flowers rising to the sun in the grip of their photosynthetic process. Warm and hopeful, they turned the sun's light into their own energy. At another point he had felt the immense, delicate, and precise magnetism of the moon's tide-pull refreshing the roots and leaves of growing things, drawing out each plant's life-flow to its very limit. There was nothing like that now on this October evening, when the plant world of the temperate zone had made ready for winter— although somewhere off in a tree root, he picked up the signal of a tiny cell not yet overcome by the season's command to sleep; the cell was still perking along, striking its endless bargain with the bacteria that helped it feed on minerals in the soil.

On the branch of a tree he found a bird dreaming of flight, and on another branch an empty-headed owl, scanning for mice with eyes that pierced the dark. A lone firefly hovered over the lawn, sending out a hopeless but single-minded phosphorescent blink, more than a month after a million other fireflies had mated and vanished. How had this lone survivor remained behind in the cooler weather? A mutant, perhaps. Ahead, inside the front wall of the inn, a newly pregnant mouse crept upward to the attic, avoiding the cat's scent and scouting for a nest to shelter her family from the coming winter.

Forrest stood on the stone terrace, turning his open mind back to the yard he had just crossed, and the cries of life from the tiny multitude rose up like a mist from the ground. Never before had he tuned to the frequency that let him hear this blending of Earth sounds in just this way, and it stopped him.

Survival was the only motif he could pick out, an urge to life both raw and blind, a one-note song; or rather, a song in which each creature's single note joined to make a chord that harmonized the pitch of each. Coming from such a genetic mold, it was no wonder that the people of Earth paid so little heed to their inner life. The fight for life itself, the rude push to keep on being them-

selves, ate them up alive, no matter how
they tried to disguise it. Evolution had softened no edges but had made the edges
harder to see. By contrast, the species-wide
memory and awareness of his own people
was not evolved but stored up, and it gave
to all an eternal warmth of feeling made up
of intimacy, wisdom, and play. How could
he possibly help Mary Alice or anyone else
who did not know what the mindstream
was?

But he had to. Things had not worked out
as he had hoped with Mary Alice and his
son, but he had to do something more for
them than leave an insurance policy.

He opened the front door of the inn, and
a bell jangled off-key somewhere in the
back of the house. He scanned, and no one
was in earshot except the tabby cat, who
lay beside the fireplace in the living room.
Behind a fire screen, the fire had caved in
safely upon its own coals, where a cherry
glow hovered amidst gray ash. The house
had fallen under a hush, and when a floor-
board creaked under Forrest's foot, he
abandoned the awkwardness of his Earth
body. With an easy wave to the wide-eyed
cat, he floated up the stairs without letting
his feet touch the steps, and he slipped into
the bedroom through a crack in the wall so
he did not have to turn the door's squeaky
hinge.

He stood at the foot of the bed, facing his sleeping wife. She had moved toward his side of the bed, and her arm reached out to rest on his pillow. The tiny dot of life inside her was sleeping also, as was its due, and growing steadily even while it slept. Yes, he owed his child a chance at the truth about who his father was. He could imprint the information even now, but a child growing up in this world with such an imprint might believe himself mad.

And then it came to him. The best way to speak to his child was by myth—and through the mother. The pressure for instant reaction on this planet made people jump to conclusions like mountain goats from one rocky peak to the next. Their minds stood in need of myths to function at all as they sought quick paths through the jungle of life. Whatever humans did not know, but wondered about or feared, could be stirred up by a myth. Life was too large, too dangerous, too varied to be grasped and interpreted except by the big idea of a myth.

A person took a myth seriously when it made him feel something about who he was (or thought he was), where he came from, and where he was going. It gained deepening power with remoteness of time or place and held that power as long as its story still shook up and bolstered the listener's own self.

A myth made people feel better when it
roused sleeping fears and then renewed
flagging hopes. The unfolding story-action
carried those feelings into a new blending
of moods where fresh hope made one freer
to act on one's life. When the hero died,
hope did not die, because the hero left
behind something of value, something that
made life better for his people. Magic often
played a part, but the story nonetheless
stalked onward with inner logic, moving its
cause-and-effect bones toward an end that
held surprise and satisfaction. There was a
rightness to a good myth: it did not tell
everything, but it told enough. And it set
fears to rest—not forever, but so that life
could go on.

He forced Mary Alice awake without speaking, and she started up in bed with a look
of alarm on her face.

"Forrest? What is it?"

"I have something to tell you." He had
made her adrenaline surge, so she would
feel the crisis, and she was fully alert now.

"I'm going to ask you to listen without
interrupting," he said, "because in a few
minutes I must leave you and go home."

She was about to speak, thinking he
meant New York, but he silenced her.
"There's no time. I'm not quite who you
think I am, and I want you to know for the

sake of our child—and also because I'm sorry that I must hurt you. In time you will find a way to tell him about me."

In quick order and with images, he showed her the history of the mindstream's hesitant and benign visits to Earth over the last half million years. Then he poured into her mind the information-images and sense-impressions that would let her see why he and his friends had come to Earth and why he had led her to love and marry him. He told her that she was only the most recent of the daughters of Man to have met up with someone who in other times would have seemed to be an angel or a god. Perhaps someday she would accept what had happened; or perhaps not. That was up to her. She knew where he was from and had tried not to think about it, but now she could avoid it no longer.

In the space of a few seconds 4-S-T finished his personal mission on Earth, using all the powers the mindstream could spare, when he told his Earthling wife:

The Myth of Red

Red is the key to what we have done. Red, the color of our planet, is on Earth the color of magic and of life. When we first came, the race that has now become human used only a few words of speech,

was weaker than its ape cousins, and had
lost its fur through some freak mutation.
They did not think us gods because they
had no gods, but they did believe in
magic and saw our acts as magical. To
this day Earthlings trust in magic even
when they fail at it, because their unconscious mind still says yes when reality and
reason say no.

On our first visit, five thousand centuries ago, we gave the secret of fire to
tribes living in hill caves in what is now
Central China, because we saw that
many ice ages would ravage the Earth in
times when the larger-brained primates
were still pitifully weak and barely capable of tribal organization. Sadly, many of
these people simply worshiped fire—
their first god—and found only a few of
the uses to which it might be put. They did
not advance the life of their species and
were finally replaced.

On another visit thirty-five thousand
years ago, twelve of our kind came here
to study Earth's cultural progress and, of
course, found almost none. An accident
trapped them here, and they made the
best of their misfortune. They sired large
families, from whose interbreeding a new
branch of the human family sprang, the
people you call Cro-Magnon. To these,
the children of the mindstream, we gave

the zodiac and the Great Bear and the
Little Bear, the latter two to help humans
find true north. By showing ourselves in
our natural form, which is something like
the bears of Earth (except that we have
hands with opposable thumbs), we made
these lessons memorable to the natives.
Bear worship came to be one of the earliest forms of religion known to mankind,
though we did not encourage this. We
also drew attention to the phases of the
moon and set down a rough calendar,
knowledge needed for civilization but
perhaps in the long run not wise. Your
dominant culture, especially in the last
two thousand years, has grown from a
principle of counting and measuring the
outer world, and it neglects and fails to
honor the boundless wealth of inner life.
The mindstream foresaw this trend and
had earlier established a shrine at Delphi
whose message to the world was "Know
thyself." This reminder of the soul, or psy-
che, was meant to counterbalance the
charms of technology, and someday the
proper balance may be restored to your
culture—but not yet. What we did not
know at that time was that the gift for
counting was built into your genes and
that this power would so easily outstrip
the impulse to self-knowledge, which
often entails deep personal pain and

must always fight against the opposing impulse to keep from knowing the truth about oneself. The counting gene tends to be dominant in most men but recessive in many women, who rightfully dismiss that ability and look for emotional penetration instead.

Farming was not one of our inventions but the discovery of many women, who knew themselves to be governed by the moon; women who felt the moon's power in growing things, who knew they could delve into the earth because Earth was also a mother. Another human triumph, the wheel, has no counterpart on Mars— we never needed it, since we had natural magnetism in our hands and feet—but on Earth the wheel broke the bonds of friction and gravity. It came about when a young girl turned a potter's round base on its edge and rolled it from one place to another because it was too heavy to carry; and then, when told to move two at once, she simply ran a pole between them and pushed the heavy burden handily—a weight no man could have carried in the usual way. She had invented the axle.

The traces of the mindstream's presence are almost beyond counting. The ancient Egyptian god Set was first portrayed as a man with red hair, later as an animal; but of course he was one of our strain. And what does Set do in your myth? He destroyed the body of Osiris, the vegetation god who prefigured Christ, and sent him to the underworld. The mindstream meant to give Earthlings a chance to develop inwardly in a way that would match their growing mastery over nature. But it was not to be: in later years the priests of Osiris regained their power and took revenge by sacrificing red-haired men each year at their dead god's shrine. The thoughtful and generous Set's effort failed; he had wanted to reduce the power of the priests, who controlled writing, record keeping, granaries, land, and the ruler's mind.

Set was also the god of Menes—his adviser, really—and Menes was the king and conqueror who vanquished the Black Kingdom in northern Egypt, where Osiris' priests held sway, and united it with his own Red Kingdom in the south, thus founding the first dynasty. Unhappily, the descendants of Menes had such a rich and easy life that they became obsessed with the idea of escaping death, and this turned their hopes once more to Osiris, who ruled the underworld and had returned from the dead. Menes was, in fact, successful in the wrong way, being less of a philosopher than we would have liked. But he became a legend of kingly power as a person who could focus the force of the state, and his name was given to other men, such as Minos, who founded an island empire. The meaning of Menes is "the steady one who prevails," and his name became a title of royalty in the ancient world, taken by many of his successors because of his godlike prestige.

In much the same way, more than three thousand years later, the name Caesar became an awesome title, one that outlasted the long hegemony of Rome. But Menes has outstripped Caesar in that his his name lives on honorably today in the homely but potent Yiddish word mensch, for which your dictionaries give the wrong derivation. In most tongues there is no single word which sums up the idea of a man in a way that calls to mind the praiseworthy traits to be looked for in all men, but the name Menes and the word mensch come close.

These terms bespeak a man who seeks first to master himself before dealing with others, who works in an honest, down-to-earth way to fulfill his life's tasks and meet his obligations to any and all, at the same time taking care to protect what is his own—whether property, family, or good name—and to support those who *depend upon him. He is a man who can feel what others feel because he keeps a clear channel to his own deepest prompt- ings; who does not lose himself in others; whose generosity is not greater than his common sense; who gives his best thoughts to those who deserve them; whose balanced soul trusts and distrusts in right measure; who is angry for just cause; who honors the life in others even when they do not; who marks his limits but is not afraid to try his hand beyond them, since in times past he has known himself to do things he doubted possible; who might forgive his wife for sleeping with another man but not for neglecting his child; who stands before no judge stricter than his own conscience and seeks no jury of peers quicker to restore his free- dom than himself in the jurisdiction of his own self-resolve; whose skeptical eye never dispraises the worth of life itself, but whose lodestone nugget of integrity stubbornly refuses to point out a track to survival that can only be reached at the cost of one's living soul. And if life and his own shortcomings force him to wear an old shirt rather than a new one, he puts it on clean.*

He knows what he does not know, and he does nothing he believes he should not do.

There is no such man on Earth, but all men glimpse the shining edges of his character when they are truest to themselves. These traits are found in women, too, of course. Fully as many stalwart women as men have walked the Earth, and most such persons have lived and died without the notice of history. The human race would not have survived were this not so.

In the myths of Earth, Odysseus stands first among heroes whom the onslaughts of a hostile world would have ruined if it were not for their native ingenuity and stout-hearted character. He wanted only to go home after a war in which he did not wish to fight—but he could not. He was a man, though he became a legend—and he had red hair. And Menelaus, the only man clever enough to trick Odysseus, also had red hair; as did the mightiest of the Achaeans, Achilles, whose boundless wrath brought Greek civilization to the brink of ruin on the plains of Troy.

Many of your own ancestors had red hair, as will our son, but I want you to understand that red hair is not important; it is no more than a clue and a reminder. The rash and foolish Esau had red hair. In that genetic experiment set in motion by one of my predecessors, Esau inherited *the hair, but his dark-haired twin, Jacob, was born with the quick mind. Esau gave up his right of succession in the lineage of the patriarchs of Israel for a bowl of red pottage (lentils from the Red Land of Egypt). Later he founded Edom, the red country east of Judah, where copper was mined, but he and his line faded from history.*

The mindstream's most rewarding intervention into life on Earth was with Moses, who surprised us by the depth of his grasp of several sensible rules of tribal life we had ordained amongst the children of the mindstream in the far past. We reminded Moses of these rules, and he used them as a kind of constitution to bind together a cultural group that even now continues to renew itself to good purpose.

Another outstanding member of our strain was the shepherd David, later king. Your Bible describes him as "ruddy," and this was true of his complexion, but his hair also marked him as one of us. We had no direct contact with him, but it was not needed: he was himself, with the best of Earth genius. As a poet he was tortured by intimations of the mindstream, which he could never imagine or share, but as a military tactician and a leader of men, his insights were drawn from the higher powers we nurtured in the children of the mindstream. And when he hurled the stone at the giant Palestinian, he knew that he had to do it and believed that he could do it, but he did not know that he guided the stone with his mind for a single deadly second.

We did not always mate with Earthlings. One expedition stayed on Earth for almost a century and inspired by direct mind probing: Confucius; the Buddha; the Persian, Zoroaster, and his Greek disciple, Pythagoras (who we sent later to study with the Celtic Druids); and Pindar, the poet of heroic personal achievement, all of whom lived roughly at the same time in far corners of the world. Jewish prophets, Greek philosophers, scientists, poets, artists—we gave them free rein.

However, in the same period, another expedition used the traditional approach: For our greatest sustained breeding effort we chose La Tène, a protected location in the center of the European continent (now Switzerland) to plant our strain so strongly among the Celts that their descendants to this day have taken red hair everywhere in the world. They overran most of northern Europe first, because we encouraged their group feeling, which is the first virtue of the mindstream. The great Arab philosopher of history, Ibn Khaldun, almost two thousand years later singled out group feeling as the decisive factor in the founding of dynasties, and he was more right than he knew. This is a natural feature of tribal life on Earth, and also of the makeup of the mindstream on Mars. However, on Earth, group feeling is inevitably lost as success allows descendants of the group to go their separate ways, whereas on Mars group feeling grows stronger with time.

In the modern era, there was Eric the Red, who sailed to the New World five centuries before another man with red hair, the deeply intuitive Jew, Christopher Columbus. And there was Queen Elizabeth I, whose cleverness kept England as a land in which the slowly developing tradition of freedom might enlarge itself; the incredibly prolific Vivaldi, whom people called the Red Priest; and in old age, why did Leonardo da Vinci, the most cunning inventor since red-haired Daedalus, draw his self-portrait in red chalk? And why the ocher handprints in the caves at Lascaux? These are memories, throwbacks to the long-standing mindstream connection with Earth. The genius Jonathan Swift somehow remembered that the home planet had two moons, and he put this fact in his novel a generation before your telescopes discovered the moons.

Rembrandt, also, was a remarkable child of the mindstream and could paint a soul within a face, with a genius verging on wizardry.

There is much else. Judas, that sweet-natured and thoughtful man of peace, is often shown in your art with red hair. He tried to save civilization from the dreadful mistake of the vegetation god in denatured form, Christ. Judas foresaw the bloody divisions of humanity that would follow the establishment of a doctrine holding that life on Earth is relevant only to the life hereafter. He wept at the fact that such a religion trivializes the tragic paradox of the human condition, but he failed, and he killed himself in anguish over that failure.

And then there was Pan, whom we sought to set up as a god practical for everybody, useful in any locality and known in all because of his devotion to the pleasures of the here and now. Pan was the "god of everything," the mythic representation of human animality and Martian mindstream. But he died under the prolonged impact of the Christ myth, leaving only his horns behind as a symbol of the Christian Satan.

In your own country's history there have been many linked to the children of the mindstream, but two will suffice:

George Washington (his hair was dark reddish and he conquered the Redcoats); and reddest of all the founding fathers of the republic, Thomas Jefferson.

Insight is not always a blessing: think of the case of poor red-bearded Vincent van Gogh. An aura of cosmic violence shimmers in his work, as if he saw into the nuclear explosions that fuel the stars and the powers that hold the atoms together and blow them apart. His talent grew wild like a weedy vine that strangles a tree, and the more he saw, the less he could bear it. In a way, his sanity drove him mad.

The very first artists were a little like him—the painters of Lascaux. When I took you to that exhibit, I had a purpose in mind: I was looking for a way to tell you about the mindstream of which I am a part, but I came at the problem crudely. The people of Lascaux were only a few generations removed from the twelve explorers who sired their kind. They had been told about the mindstream, and they were anxious to tap its power; the cave at Lascaux was a stumbling effort to reproduce a mindstream of their own as a circling cloud of images. Brilliant, but a universe away from the reality. It gave a moment's good group feeling, but in the long run it was much more exciting for a group of men to chase and kill the ani-

mals they meant to eat. Group feeling can only be heightened by group action, and the cave rituals palled at last.

Our history has traces of an older race that visited us even as we have visited you. The mindstream has hovered over Earth like a guardian angel now and again for many ages, paying its tribute to the life of this planet. It must now withdraw. We leave as hesitantly as we came, but we leave nevertheless. One curious irony in the relation between Mars and Earth is that your kind is stronger than ours in the structure of genes. Perhaps the early genetic material evolved under harsher pressures here; or perhaps your nature has been hardened by the ongoing battle against death; or maybe the clear-cut division into two genders, which is so hard for us to understand, has somehow added to your strength. But what is hardest of all to grasp is that no human seems able to believe that he will die, often even when he is actually dying. There may be a clue in the words of one of your philosophers: "Scimus et sentimus nos immortales esse." "We know and feel that we are immortal."

The mindstream knows immortality because all of us experience it when our spirits survive bodily death—but why should humans feel this way when all die *and none return? Your feeling is involuntary, unconscious, direct, and universal; it is a psychological truth beyond your control. Perhaps it also means something you may yet discover.*

Another clue: In the words of a more recent thinker, "The unconscious is immortal." The source of lasting art, penetrating ideas, and all hope is not everyday experience but humanity's unconscious mind. Out of its dark confines comes the light you must have in order to live; and it may be that the human race has not yet lived long enough to discover its own true nature.

Martians have no unconscious mind, so perhaps . . .

There was much more, as Forrest interwove the history of Mars with the uneven development of the human race, right down to the expedition that brought him to Earth. No matter what the mindstream had done here, it led to further conflict and struggle rather than to peace. That seemed to be the human lot. At the very last, he said:

This I tell you to understand and remember: Your child's life is both a farfetched miracle and a hard fact. I promise you that he will be superb.

Never believe otherwise.

. . .

All this took but a few seconds to make known to Mary Alice, who had come bolt upright in bed.

"Forrest," she said shakily, "I can't believe a word you're saying."

I know

he replied. He said this in the same way he had narrated the Myth of Red.

but notice that I did not use words I spoke only within your mind

She stared at him, her face not yet showing the shock that would come soon enough when she began to believe. This reality had to be first denied because it was too painful.

There was nothing else for him to do. He had to meet the others where the spacecraft was about to touch down, and he adjusted himself to fade. Mary Alice covered her face with her hands, and he could feel the shock shooting through her body. He hesitated. Had he forgotten anything? Yes, of course. With a quick flick of his mind he pushed the rowboat away from the dock so that it would float out onto the lake and be found empty at daybreak. His phantom likeness still shimmered in the room.

"Wait!" Mary Alice cried out, and he steadied himself so that he remained visible, though he knew she could see through his body to the curtains gently fluttering at the window behind him. Her face told him that she was on the verge of belief, though she still fought the truth. Inside her mind he made a vision of the home planet, red and welcoming, and the singing of the others, excited and eager to return. It was brutal, but the honesty of it would help her in time. Rough truth was better than a smooth lie, and the clean wound would make healing start quickly.

"I need more," she whispered, too frightened to weep. "Something to show our child." He could feel her rising panic; she was ready to scream, ready to rage in helplessness at his abandonment of her.

A possibility came to him for what she needed, and he swiftly implanted the necessary knowledge in her mind. The details would be waiting for the moment when they would come to her unbidden, like inspiration, and she would have what she asked.

He nodded and raised his hand in farewell. Mary Alice screamed and reached out toward his melting image, as if to hold him with a touch. But the room was empty, and she was alone.

A moment later in Sheep Meadow in Central Park, a curious thing took place. Afterward it made a story in the newspapers for a day or two and was then forgotten, though not by Mary Alice. At first she had run through the inn, crying and banging doors until Madame laid hands on her and held her gently, until she stopped shaking and wept quietly. In the hours after Forrest vanished, she lay in bed, tears streaming, unable to tell anyone what she knew. He was really gone, but she could not accept it. After she wept, she went into a fury again and threw the coffee mug and the volume of de Maupassant out the window. *How dare he?*

How dare he do this to her? Make her love him, use her sexually, make her pregnant, then leave almost without saying good-bye? Madame had spoken soothingly and tucked her into bed, but Mary Alice was too angry for any gentle comfort. In the dark before dawn, she came up with the perfect revenge: she would kill his child; she would get an abortion. Vengeance swirled hot and bloody in her mind, but after a quarter hour of savoring the idea, imagining a tiny smeared fetus plucked from her body, she knew she could not do it. The child was hers, too, and in fact, it would be *all* hers now that Forrest was gone.

And the child was conceived in love, at least so far as her feelings were concerned, and she wanted it. She might hate Forrest, but she would have the child because it was hers. Her anger rose and fell like an ocean tide, out of her control, but in the end she came back to her pregnancy, to the life within her. That life was precious, there was no question but that she would have the baby, and that was that. As the sun came up, the thought occurred to her that she could not harbor a hidden hatred for Forrest, because it would be unfair to the child, who had to feel a decent regard for both parents, even for the one who had gone away.

Mary Alice knew herself too well to believe that she had imagined or dreamed the recounting of the myth, and she remembered in detail all that Forrest had said and how he said it. She could repeat it word for word, if need be.

Later a sheriff's deputy came and questioned her, then dragged the lake all day at the inn as she watched from her window, but Mary Alice knew the body would never be found.

Back in the city, she read about the curious event in Sheep Meadow and somehow she understood that she had to go to Central Park and see the spot that had been burned bare by an odd electrical storm on the night Forrest had vanished. What had brought her there she could not say—there was nothing much to see—but as she turned to leave the patch of scorched earth, the toe of her shoe touched something that gleamed like crystal. She knelt and dislodged the object from the yielding earth and held it in her hand. It was surprisingly warm to her fingers and had the appearance of a piece of fused glass; but as she brushed the earth away she saw that it was highly polished, and as she looked more closely she recognized the shape of a tiny bear, like the sandbears in the pink deserts of Mars.

She came slowly to her feet, still holding the bear. It was very important, but she was not quite sure of how and why. Mary Alice had not yet grasped what her own life would be in the years to come, but the life growing in her womb was her own to bear, and she would protect it. Or *him,* as Forrest had said. She stood, not moving, for a long time and studied the little bear, until at last under the warmth of her questioning gaze the bear's eyes gleamed at her, and a voice spoke within her mind:

never believe otherwise

3
—

From somewhere beyond the moon, 4-S-T
heard the echo of the message he had im-
planted and knew that all was well. He had
lied to her at first, but in the end he had told
her the truth, and perhaps in time she would
not hate him. She would keep the crystal
bear, and it would speak to her when she
yearned for hope, or needed reassurance.
Free at last, he looked down on Earth, a
sharp-edged bluish disk streaked with white
swirling clouds, floating improbably in the
midst of the bleakness of space. The others
had gone into hibernation now for the re-
turn voyage, but he stayed awake to catch
all the sense impressions he could. Earth's
face looked serene as he gazed at it
through the porthole, but up close he knew

it to be a dangerous place. Yet it remained oddly appealing; in spite of the nerve-wracking violence, it was an outpost of life, an oasis of growing things surrounded by the wasteland of the cosmos. The space-craft gained speed rapidly, and the blue disk grew smaller against the barren and overpowering immensity of space.

And then he heard it, the immortal sound of the planet.

He had tuned himself once more to the frequency that he had discovered a few hours earlier as he looked out over the lawn for the last time at the inn. Up from the spinning blue globe rose a cloud of music, a dominant, complex chord that beamed out through the void like the beacon of a lighthouse. He marveled at it. How had he missed it—how had they all missed it—before? The sound charmed and puzzled him, and he let himself wonder about it even in his present lonely state, cut off for a time from the mindstream and the friendly feelings of the others now asleep. It seemed to him that the groundless optimism of living things on that strange planet must somehow have its source in their form of matter it-self—that had to be the answer. Earth pro-toplasm was one thing, but perhaps in the universe at large each electron was a tri-umph, each photon a bearer of life, stars an incredible conquest, and mind a total victory. Filling the emptiness of space, however that was done, and no matter how small the region occupied, defeated that emptiness for a time. Acting on this bone-deep knowledge, the riotous creatures of Earth would outlast their dilemmas, their enemies, perhaps even their discordant and disorderly selves.

He had missed this thrilling resonance until today, and none of them had heard it on their approach to Earth five months ago. Then they had slept through the first crossing to save energy for Earth tasks and woke only when they were about to land. They had feared this mission, with good cause, and had almost let its chief treasure, the singing, go unnoticed.

For this little world was singing. From its living chemicals, the viruses, to its stately trees and the whole kingdom of green life, to the thronging fishes of the sea and the angelic birds of the air, to the beasts of the field, to the jungle, to the restless-minded family of mankind—all these billions of transmitters of the spark of life raised dire cries of their condition; all had their say, and voices without number merged into a vast singing, a single sustained note that came on cheerful as sunrise. Taken singly, each spirit was too weak to radiate its lonely message to any distance; but somehow all joined in at this frequency so that many voices in a minor key shaded into a swelling song of triumph.

Now he would not sleep but would listen to the harmony of this planet's creation for as far as he could make it out, so that when it was too faint to hear, he would at last be able to bring back, for the eternal delight of the mindstream, the joyful noise of the singing of Earth.